DAUGHTER OF A HOOD LEGEND 2

LATOYA NICOLE

Daughter of a Hood Legend 2

Copyright © 2018 by LaToya Nicole

Published by Mz. Lady P Presents

"Everywhere I'm looking now, I'm surrounded by your embrace. Baby I can see your halo, you know you're my saving grace. You're everything I need and more, it's written all over your face. Baby I can feel your halo you know you're my saving grace." Halo- Beyonce

My daughter has been my saving grace without even know it. She has brought me so much joy, and all that matters in this world is her. No one could ever fathom how I feel about her, but I try to explain it every book. So many people have turned their back on her. Treat her like she has the plague, but her uniqueness is what makes her beautiful. You don't have to understand her, just sit back and let her fill your heart with love. My Miracle Monet Riley. An angel walking the earth. My everything. I will forever be grateful, and as long as I have breath in my body, I will give you the world. I love you babes.

Acknowledgments

Every book I try to acknowledge everyone that has been so much to me. Just know as a whole, I am forever grateful to all of you. If I forget to acknowledge your name, know it's not intentional, and there is always next book. Lol I love my support team so much, just know you are the reason that I am me.

To my bookie boos, it's so much said about this group, but you have given so many people so much help and support, I appreciate the hell out of you. The challenges, spotlights, take overs, promo days all of that helps and just know Latoya Nicole appreciate yall.

Law aka Bestie you are something else. You give me hell, but you keep it real and that's all a friend can ask for. I'm proud of you and all of your accomplishments. You are doing so much and I want you to keep pushing forward no matter how hard it gets. You got this and don't you ever forget it.

ZaTasha, I don't know another way I can tell you thank you, but I will try. You never tell me know and I will forever be grateful for that. I am probably the hardest person to test read for, but you do it with a smile never getting mad no matter what madness I take you through. I love you and I appreciate you bae. Don't ever forget that.

Krissy you just took a spot in my life. Thank you for being there for me no matter what time it is. I love you and thank you for helping me make sure my book is great.

Kb Cole your ass been missing in action, but I know what it is. I love you and my niece and I appreciate you being my friend. You are amazing, and I love you. Yall check out her catalog.

A.J Davidson your ass helped me so much, I thank you for being there. I don't know where I would have been without you. I appreciate you cousin for having my back. You're a great person and an amazing author. Yall check out her catalog. Welcome baby Andrew aka baby apple I can't wait to meet you.

Annitia chile you are just awesome. I love ya girl and keep pushing. I'm glad you chose me to be your AG.

Fay, Monisha, Victoria, Kady, Franny, Kanice I love you squad all day.

To my family Steph, Malik, Johnnae, Shunta, Shenitha, Sheketta, Sheena, Antronna, Jennifer, Ebony Bae… thank yall for supporting me no matter what. I love yall.

A.M Thank you for allowing me back into your life. You are an amazing friend and I am happy to share my gift with you. You push me and I will forever be grateful to you. Don't ever change who you are.

WHERE WE LEFT OFF...

"I love you too." Closing my eyes, I fell asleep while he played in my hair.

My ass went to sleep too early and now I was woke looking stupid. Seeing that it was only nine at night, I left him sleeping peacefully and went home. I wasn't playing games this time. I was going home to tell my daddy about us. It was time for me to stop hiding and be happy. My daddy was gone have to accept this was who I loved.

All the way home, I sung love songs. I hated that we missed all that time together all because I was playing games and shit. I was new to this shit and I was learning, but I was going to do better. Pulling up to the house, I got out with a new purpose. This was going to be a great thing, I could feel it. When I walked inside, my daddy was sitting in the front drinking.

He looked like he aged ten years since the last time I saw him. I felt bad for not being there for him like I should have. He lost his brother and I was too busy trying to cover my own ass. I couldn't let him find out who I was, so I stayed away scared he would see right through me.

"Hey daddy, are you okay? I miss you." Sitting down next to him, I hugged him tight.

"I'm good. It's time we talk. I need to tell you about twenty two years ago. I've been keeping you hostage because I didn't want you to date the same type of nigga as me. You've always known that, but you don't know the nigga I was. It's

time for me to let you be grown and make your own decisions. If you know everything, you will know to make the right ones based off the mistakes I made." He was starting to scare me, but I dared not interrupt him. He may stop talking and I needed to know this story. I've been trying to get this out of him for twenty years and he would never tell me.

"Twenty two years ago, the love of my life went into labor and blew my phone up. I didn't answer because I was out there in the streets. A street nigga don't know how to separate the two. The deal I was about to make would set us up for life, so I chose to ignore her call and handle business.

Mind you, I didn't know she was in labor. So while I'm with the connect, we make the deal. He told me in order for him to honor it, I had to sleep with one of his women. I had never cheated on your mother, but I wanted this deal bad as fuck in order to make sure your mama never wanted for nothing.

Against my better judgement, I slept with the woman. When I left out, me and Fat Back was celebrating the deal when my phone rang again. This time it was the nurse. When I got there, she was already dead. If I had not been there sleeping with that bitch, I probably could have saved her. Maybe she wouldn't have been stressed. It was so much guilt inside me, I felt I had been dealt instant karma. While I was sleeping with this bitch, my wife died. After I made sure you were good, I went back to Vega's house." Sitting up, I was confused.

"Daddy, who is Vega?"

"Capone, he was the connect that had me sleep with the bitch. Anyway, I went back to his house and killed anything standing. The bitch I fucked was gone, but I killed that nigga. His son was in there with him, but I left him alive. I couldn't bring myself to kill his baby. See, I felt odd when I left his office like he had some type of trick up his sleeve. I couldn't prove it, but what I did know was if I wasn't fucking that bitch, I would have been with my wife. To me, it was his fault. After that, I walked away from the streets and never looked back. Find you a man that is going to be better than I was. When they are in the streets, nine times out of ten they are going to be just like me.

We are going to do anything to make a major deal happen, even if it means fucking over our family. I know you probably hate me, but I want you to walk away from this story knowing what it means to be with a street nigga. I know that's what you like, but it's not worth it." He had no idea the shock that went through my body. The man that he killed, was Capone's father. All this time, this nigga was using me to avenge his father's death. This bitch ass nigga was using me. Trying to stay calm, I looked at my daddy and eased his mind.

"You're the realest nigga I know. I could never hate you and you are still my hero. I love you daddy, stop beating yourself up. I'm okay and I'm glad you told me the story. Let that guilt go sus, mama wouldn't want that."

"Don't get your ass knocked out talking about sus. I'll slap your ass to sleep." Laughing, I stood up to leave.

"I'm going to head back to Boo's house. I'll check on you in the morning okay?" He looked at me strange and stood to hug me.

"You sure you're okay baby girl?"

"Yeah daddy, I'm good. We're good, I promise." Walking out, I made sure both of my guns were loaded and headed back to Capone's house. He wanted Roulette, well he was about to get her. He knew who the fuck my daddy was, I couldn't believe his ass tried me. This was going to be a lesson he learned the hard way. The Roulette way.

When I pulled up, I knew it was all or nothing. Getting out, I raised my guns and started firing. Knocking down the guards one by one, I made sure I gave all head shots. Going through the house, I continued shooting my way through until I found him. He was standing at his desk looking shocked when I raised my gun at him.

"Tell me Capone. Are you feeling lucky?"

Chapter One

ROULETTE

Standing with my gun pointed at Capone, I looked at him with tears in my eyes. My heart was hurting and I wanted this nigga to pay. Breezy and Glitch was right, this nigga played me. I'm supposed to be a boss and I was around here acting like a sprung ass bitch who didn't know any better. Not anymore, he had me fucked up. This nigga chose to play with his life, and he picked the right person for the job. My name was Roulette, I'm the queen of that shit.

None of this made sense, but at this point, I didn't give a fuck about nothing except making him suffer. I wanted him to watch me kill him slowly. What was pissing me off the most, was the confused look on his face. It's as if he didn't think I would find this shit out. Yeah, his bitch ass confessed his love to me, but that does not make up for all the lies this nigga told.

"Capone Vega." He looked at me like I was crazy, but I had to say it out loud to accept who this nigga was. "Capone fucking Vega. Bitch ass nigga took my virginity like my shit meant nothing. Square nose having ass nigga. How the fuck do you smell? I been meaning to ask your Jeanie in a bottle body having ass. Capone fucking Vega." My ass was pacing back and forth losing my mind.

"Why do u keep saying my name? You acting like I lied to you on who I am? You know who the fuck I am."

"DO I? Did I know that you was setting me up this entire time? Did I know you was on some get back shit? Did I fucking know that you was using me bitch? TELL ME, WHAT THE FUCK DID I KNOW. Should have known not to trust a nigga that got feet in the shape of a V. You can't do shit but cross a bitch. Slip and slide ass nigga."

"Shorty…" Not wanting to hear shit else, I pulled the trigger. I shot him in the leg, so that I could work my way up to his head. "Shorty, please listen to me." Pulling the trigger again, I shot him in the stomach. As he tried to ball up, I shot his ass in the chest. Nobody would ever play me and think shit was sweet. Pointing the gun at his head, I cried as I got ready to pull the trigger. The doors bust open and I was surrounded by guards with guns drawn.

"Put the gun down." Some big Heavy D looking ass nigga yelled. If it was me and my boss was on the floor, I would have shot whoever was holding the gun and asked questions later.

"Let her go." Capone spoke above a whisper. His raggedy ass was coughing up blood trying to talk and they looked at him like he lost his mind. Seeing they didn't lower their guns, he tried his best to yell. "LET HER GO." Watching their guns lower, I backed out of there nice and slow. Never dropping my gun, I kept it pointed until I was no longer in visibility. Realizing I just kicked off a war, I took off running. Not because I was scared, but because I was on hostile territory and my ass was low on ammunition. Jumping in my car, I damn near pissed on myself seeing Vicious sitting in the passenger seat.

"Hey daddy, what are u doing here?" When he flexed his jaws, I knew shit was all bad.

"Drive." Doing as I was told, I flew like a bat out of hell to get out of there. My mind was working over time trying to figure out what to tell this Mortal Kombat looking ass nigga. Look like his ass about to scream out get over here any minute. When we got far enough, he hit the dash board so hard, I thought he punched my ass. "Pull over Kalina." Doing as I was told, my ass was shaking realizing that nothing else was around us. "You are going to tell me what the fuck is going on, and I want to know the truth."

"The truth about what daddy?" I tried to see how much he knew before I started telling on myself. A bitch was slow, but I wasn't nigga beat my ass slow.

"Kalina, I will knock your ass cross eyed if you continue to play with me. Why were you at the connect's house?"

"If you do that, how I'm gone drive us home? You crazy." I tried to give off a nervous laugh, but his ass wasn't having that. Knowing I had no choice, I closed my legs making sure he couldn't kick me in the pussy as I told him everything. "Okay, I was on my way home to tell you I was in love with my boyfriend. Before you say anything else, just know it's over now. Anyway, as you were talking about the connect you killed, you said his name. You said Capone Vega and that's the nigga's name I was fucking with. I went there to kill him. I lit his ass up and now I'm sure they are coming after me." I tried to play cry, but his ass bypassed them tears.

"Kalina, how did you meet him? Did they approach you? You have to tell me everything in order for me to help you." This was the part I was trying to avoid.

"Not exactly." Giving me the look that told me I better start talking, I said the one thing I've been keeping from him all these years. "They reached out to Roulette. They had no idea that it was me. When I showed up, we started doing business and then we started dating." Throwing my hands over my face, I tried my best to cover up just in case he one two'd my ass.

"How in the fuck are you Roulette? You go to school and come home every day." The dumb look on my face let him know that I been lying. Grabbing me around my neck, I could tell my daddy wasn't in there. For a brief moment, I thought he was going to kill me. Clawing at his hands, I tried my best to get a word out. "Daddy." For a moment, I thought he didn't hear me. Out of nowhere he let me go. His eyes turned back to normal and I was ready to beat his ass. He didn't have to do me like that, I'm his damn child.

"Kalina, when this shit is over, so is this lil game you're playing. There will be no more Roulette. If I find out your ass is anywhere near a fucking trap house, I'm going to have a velvet box made especially for you."

"Daddy, you have to understand what you are asking me. It's not just me out here, I have a crew to feed. You of all people know who I am and how I have no control over that. The shit is in my blood. I know this is a lot to take in and I'm sorry for lying to you, but I'm your daughter through and through. I can't help what runs in my veins." You could tell he was mad, but his face softened. No matter what, he knew I was right. There was nothing I could do to stop what was inside of me. This shit wasn't going nowhere and I honestly didn't want it to.

"I'm going to set up a meeting tomorrow with the crew. We are about to be at war and they need to be prepared. You fucked up and now I have to fix it. There is so much bad blood between us and you went and dropped it like it's hot for the enemy. I should slap your ass to sleep. Drive."

"With all due respect daddy, these are my streets and you not running shit. I'll set up a meeting, and out of respect for who you were, I'll allow you to attend. Don't get this shit twisted though, you're retired." His ass laughed, but I could see him clenching his jaws. I know he wanted to knock my ass out, but it was no time for a power struggle. In this moment, he was under me. Whether he liked it or not. Pulling up to the house, he got out and looked at me.

"How the fuck you running the streets and you can't even fuck right? First time you fuck you slip your ass right on the enemy. Dumb ass, go your simple ass to bed. Talking about you running shit. You better run your ass to your room before I forget you my damn daughter." Laughing, I walked past him and shrugged my shoulders. His ass could pretend to be mad all he want, but we both know his ass liked how I bossed up on his ass. I had a smile on my face, until I took my ass upstairs to my room. The shit hit me out of nowhere and all I could do was cry.

Why didn't I see the signs? How did he know my daddy would

never tell me? So many questions, and so much heartbreak. My ass decide to finally give up the pussy and got played on my first go around. Fuck niggas and fuck love. I'm going to the store to get me another Chip. I never wanted to feel this shit again and I wasn't. I hope that nigga died. If not, I would make sure to finish the job.

Chapter Two

VICIOUS

*W*hen Kalina went running out of the house, I jumped in my truck and followed her. Realizing where she was headed once we got close, I thought she crossed me. How the fuck could my daughter be fucking with the enemy. Parking my truck a couple of blocks away, I made my way to the Vega's compound. Seeing that security was already laid out, I had no problems getting in their gate. Not knowing what she was in there to do, I got in her car and waited for her to come out.

One look at me, she almost shitted on herself. The way she was acting, I thought I was gone have to relieve her brain of some pressure. I didn't give a fuck who you were, if you crossed me that ass was dead. Imagine my surprise as I found out her real secret. All this time, she was Roulette. So many emotions ran through me. First anger, and I acted on that anger. When my hands went around her neck, I blanked out. It wasn't until I heard her barely say daddy that brought me back. It was damn near inaudible, but the sound of my child's voice brought me back to my senses. After the anger subsided, I began to feel proud. Even though I hadn't taught her shit, she was running these streets as if she was me. My baby girl had the world shook and it wasn't because of me. If it wasn't for this fuck up, she would have been flawless.

Even though I tried to keep the shit from her, the shit ran through her veins and I had to accept it. My daddy didn't want me taking over his business, but it happened anyway. The more he tried to keep it me from it, the harder I fought towards it. When he saw how natural the shit came to me, he could no longer resist it. I was gone have to do the same with Kalina.

Had I known that she was gone go this route regardless, I would have stayed my ass in the game. I wasn't hiding from the Vega's. Once you cut off the head, the body will fall. I had no idea his son would come seeking revenge. His mama should have told him who the fuck I was though. He was about to endure the worst war these streets has ever seen. My nigga was gone behind this shit and now I knew who was responsible for it.

Kalina thought she was in charge, but these will always be my streets. I'm gone make her think she in charge and ride back seat. The last thing I want to do is have the streets thinking she can't handle her business. On the forefront, it will be Roulette running the show. Behind that shit, Vicious and his crew will be doing damage. I had a lot of velvet boxes to use, and I couldn't wait. Jumping in my car, I headed towards the city. Knowing I was back, the air even felt different. It was power in this concrete and the shit was intoxicating.

Sending out a group text, I told my crew to meet at the old spot 911. Most of them retired with me, some dipped in the life here and there, some just fucked their life completely up. Like Freeno. I know they were trying to figure out what the fuck was going on, but they would be there. When Vicious call, you come. No questions asked. Pulling up to an old warehouse we had back in the day, I parked and exhaled. It was our meeting spot and where we handled most of our business.

In a way, I was a little bit nervous. I know the shit was in me, but what if niggas didn't fear me like they had before? What if they look at me as some old washed up ass nigga trying to reclaim some shit? I know what I was to these streets, but times have changed. Hell, they allowed Kalina to run them without even knowing who she was. They had no idea she was my daughter and allowed her ass to reign supreme. I'm still shocked at that shit. How the fuck do you fear someone you can't see?

Seeing everyone pulling up, I shook off these feelings and got out. Right now wasn't the time for doubt, I needed to get a handle on this shit before my daughter got killed out there. A war from revenge was the worst kind, they were dealing with emotions. If you're fighting over territory, it's not personal.

"Hey Vicious, who the fuck done brought your ass out of retirement? I hope your old ass can still carry a gun and shit." Laughing at my nigga Grew, I walked up on him.

"You want to find out? Just because you can't hold your dick straight while you piss, don't mean the rest of us fucked up." Walking away pissed, I laughed and dapped up the rest of the crew. His ass hated when we joked about that shit. No matter what was going on, his ass couldn't piss right to save his life. His ass would always walk away with droplets on his hands and clothes. That's why nobody every shook up with that nigga. Walking inside, I allowed everyone to get settled in.

"I know everyone is trying to figure out why I called you all here. I'm not one to beat around the bush, so let's get to it. I'm sure you all been hearing about this Roulette nigga running the streets. Well, it turns out that Roulette is my daughter." The shocked looks came first, and then the laughs.

"Wait, how the fuck do you not know your daughter is basically you out in these streets. You were the king out there and nobody could get shit past you, but you got duped by your own damn daughter. Nigga I will never let you live this shit down." E Way was doing the most, but he was right. That's half the reason I feel I fell off. How did I miss something this big?

"Shut the fuck up. Anyway, she started dating this nigga Capone. Capone Vega." I allowed it to sink in and I no longer had to explain the situation. They knew exactly what I did twenty two years ago and they knew what we were up against. "We're going to war gentlemen, but it's a catch. We have to make Roulette I mean

Kalina feel that she is the one in charge. I don't want to make her crew feel as if she is bowing down to me or only has her status because of my name. She worked hard to get where she is and I don't want to ruin that for her. Now, remember this is only on the surface. Behind the scenes, we fix her mess."

"Your ass is Vicious for real. You done came back from the dead to take over your daughter's organization. That's some hard core shit. You're worse than ever." I laughed, but in my mind I thought about what Grew said. I never really said it out loud, but in my heart I knew I was going to take over at some point. Giving the shit up was done to keep her away, now that she is in the streets anyway, why not go back?

It will crush her to know that I'm coming back, but I've had a taste of this shit and there is no turning back now. I know that at some point, it's going to cause a rift between me and Kalina. The shit was fucking with me, but it was something she would have to understand. I figure, I'll run my side and she run hers.

If she don't want to do it that way, then we allow the streets to decide. I didn't want to do that to her, because they will pick me. I hope this war allows her to see that this is not the life she wants to live. In the meantime, I would ride the backseat until this shit was over.

Chapter Three

CAPONE

*E*veryone around me was screaming and panicking. I was still trying to wrap my mind around what happened. Not that Roulette shot me, but the why was bothering me. It's like she was accusing me of something, but I have no idea what the fuck she was talking about. My life was slipping from me and all I could think about was what the fuck did I do wrong.

"We have to wait for his mother to come. If we take him to the hospital, they will ask too many questions. If that's not what she wants, all of our ass will be fired." My security was trying to figure out how to keep their jobs, meanwhile I was losing my life. This had to be the most ignorant shit I ever heard in my fucking life.

"Fuck that. I'm not doing shit until she answers her fucking phone. I need my job. I got another shorty on the way."

"Damn nigga, how many you got now? It has to be like ten. Your ass shooting them bitches out ain't you?"

"Fuck you. It ain't my fault I'm potent." I had enough. Reaching behind my back, I tried my best to grab my gun. Pointing it at the ceiling, I shot it off.

"Boss man what the fuck" They all rushed over to me.

"Exactly. I'm the boss and if you don't get me to the fucking hospital, I will kill all of you right here, right now. How the fuck are you going to leave me here dying waiting on my damn mama?" My ass was damn near whispering, but they knew I meant business. They had this shit fucked up and I was their boss, not her. Grabbing me up, they carried me out to the car. It was blood everywhere and I knew I didn't have long.

Knowing their lives were on the line, they ass was moving so fast they were fucking me up. They almost dropped me, niggas hit my head against the door, and basically just tossed my ass in the truck. Now they were driving like crazy and hitting every damn bump on the road. I wanted to tell they ass to just pull over and let me out. Taking my chances on the side of the road had to be better than this shit. I was in so much pain and these fools were scared out of their minds. I've never been happier to see a hospital in all of my life. When they opened the door to carry me out, I almost told they ass I got it. Ain't no way I could walk, but I would damn sure try if it meant getting away from their incompetent asses.

Finally I was taken on a stretcher and being rushed into surgery. The lights were fading and I could feel myself going. Every blink was becoming harder and I knew my time was coming. Ironically, all I could think about was Roulette. I needed her to know how I felt before I died. My body was too weak to tell someone to call her, and it finally went black.

Waking up, it was beeping and machines everywhere. My body was sore and I could barely move. The lights were bright and I tried to turn my head to see if anyone was here. My heart hoped I would see Roulette and she could tell me what the fuck happened, but I was alone. Hearing footsteps, I got hopeful that she went and got some snacks and was now on her way back in the room. Trying my best to turn my head, I was pissed to see I made all that effort for Shitz. Closing my eyes, I tried to pretend like I was sleep. All I wanted to do was talk to Roulette to find out what the fuck happened.

"Nigga quit trying to play sleep, I saw you see me see you. How the fuck you look me dead in the eyes and then play sleep?" Smiling, I opened my eyes. It was a long shot, but maybe he wasn't really paying attention.

"My bad." My throat was dry as hell. Noticing how scratchy my voice was, he handed me the water.

"This what your shorty for. I'm not a bed nurse. Where the fuck she been anyway? Your ass been out for a week and I had to leave a lot of shit just so somebody can be here for your weak neck ass." Hearing him say that triggered something inside of me. I been out for a week and my mama hasn't even been to see me. Something about that didn't sit right with me. For whatever reason, I know why Roulette wasn't here. She was mad at me about something, but my mama, that's a different story.

"Shorty the one that put me here." This nigga looked shocked and then dead ass started laughing.

"Wait. You telling me Roulette the one that shot your ass up? What the fuck you do to her?" Shrugging my shoulders the best way I could, I was just as lost as him.

"I don't know. She just kept saying my name and said I lied to her. I haven't done shit, so I don't know what the fuck is going on."

"You want me to go air her ass out. All you have to do is say the word and her ass is gone."

"Naw, I don't want you to do shit. You can tell me why my mama haven't been up here to see me though."

"She waved that boujie ass hand at me and told me to handle it. I don't think she is handling it well. You know people panic in different ways. She seems to not want to deal with it as if it never happened." Shit still seemed off to me and there was no excuse. If my child got his ass lit up, I would be there no matter what.

"I need you to get in touch with Roulette. There a lot of questions that I need answered and only she can give me that."

"Bro fuck her. She wanted a war, well, she got one. You don't need a woman that is willing to kill you. No matter what the reason is."

"If anyone goes near her, they have to answer to me. Trust me, you have not seen a monster until you go against me. I'm down now, but nigga when I rise the fuck up, I will tear this bitch up. Don't try me. Do what the fuck I asked and do it now. You can see yourself out."

"Nigga get some unused pussy and lose they fucking mind. I'll do what you want because you my nigga, but you can keep the threatening shit. You know don't shit move on me but my piece. Get you some sleep, you done obviously lost your mind and need the rest."

"I haven't lost shit. Just remember what the fuck I said. If you go near her other than what the fuck I asked, you answer to me and you don't want that. Now like I said two minutes ago, get the fuck out and go do what I asked." The nigga actually rolled his eyes, but he knew not to fuck with me. I was a laid back type of nigga, but I was deadly. My approach is just different from most. I'm no Vicious, but I wasn't far from him. I just moved behind the scenes. I needed her to make her way up here and fast. If she thought I was against her, a war was coming and I was laid up in this bitch not able to do shit. I needed to figure out what the fuck she was pissed about so I can fix it.

"Hello Mr. Vega. I'm about to give you some morphine for the pain. It may make you sleepy, but you will feel a lot better when you wake up."

"Thank you nurse." After pushing the meds through my IV, I was out five minutes later. My last thought was Roulette.

Chapter Four

BREEZY

*S*unshine blue skies, please go away.
    My girl has found another and gone away.
With her went my future, my life is filled with gloom.
Day after day, I stay locked up in my room.
I know to you, it might sound strange.
Oh I wish it would rain.

"Bitch if you don't get out of my house with this sad ass old ass music. Shit sound like you standing on a bridge ready to fucking jump. I can't take this type of shit two times in one fucking year. I've been on that bridge and baby, I don't want to stand on that mother fucker no more." Roulette ass was over here crying and singing all the saddest music she could find. Hiding out in my room, I tried to stay away from her but enough was enough. They had my ass out there in mix match shoes to pull me out of my funk.

"Best friend, he played me and the shit hurts. Your depression was different. Warranted, but different. I have to walk through my city looking like the girl that was supposed to be a boss but got played by a nigga. I'm ruined."

"Get the fuck over it. Niggas been playing bitches since the beginning of time. You do know that it was a hoe in the bible. Who you think turned her the fuck out?" She looked at me like it made sense. Shrugging my shoulders, I laughed. "I know it's weird how right I be sometimes ain't it?"

"Yeah you're right, but I still never thought it would be me. You can talk all the shit you want, but that shit was foul and a bitch heart is in her socks." Looking down at her feet, I shook my head.

"Bitch you ain't got on socks. Get your ass the fuck up and let's go to this meeting. We have to figure out what the fuck we gone do about this shit. If he's dead like you think, we have to strike his mama and them while he's vulnerable."

"We're going to the meeting, but it's something else I need to tell you. Vicious knows that I'm Roulette, but I haven't told him about you yet. He choked my ass out, so you might want to wear a turtle neck or something. Oh, and he's going to be at the meeting." If I was drinking or eating anything, my ass would be choking.

"You been in my house all fucking day but didn't tell me that? Are you crazy? Email me the fucking plans, I'm staying my ass here. You got me fucked up, I'm not going against Vicious." I was looking for her ass to tell me she got this, but her ass looked just as shooked as me.

"Bestie, what if we have to go to war with my daddy? You know damn well his ass is not going to come back to the game and let me run it. This is about to be a mess and I'm not sure if I'm ready for this." Thinking it over, I decided to throw all caution to the wind.

"Fuck him. Don't get me wrong, if we have to go to war with Uncle V, bitch I'm a retired hoe. Fuck that, you not about to send me off but we not bowing out. You're going to run your streets and show him why it's okay for him to sit his ass at home like he been doing. Let's make his ass a Facebook page, that shit will keep him busy for hours. Don't that nigga like to read? Add him to that damn Bookies group. It's a bunch of books and freaky bitches that do BAD on Fridays." We both laughed at the thought.

"He would be appalled at the shit they talk about. You know his ass old school. Finding him a bitch would be nice though. His ass didn't hover as much when he was fucking Lisa. Let's get through the meeting first, and then we can talk about getting my daddy laid. Eeww, that shit don't sound right. We are not about to talk about my daddy's sex life. Let's go." She was right, the shit sounded nasty but I was really willing to try anything.

"I'm happy to be Breezy today. I would not want to be in your shoes."

"At least they some bad ass shoes." Looking down at her Chanel sneakers, I had to agree. Walking out of the door, we headed towards the warehouse. Glitch already left and I think Roulette ran his ass out of here with all the howling she was doing. Looking over at her, I wish I could take her pain away. My friend has never gone through this and I'm sure it was tearing her apart. I've done this dance a couple of times before, that's why I'm so grateful for Glitch. His ass stood by me until I got my shit together and he loves me flaws and all. I thought my friend had found that as well, instead she is sitting over there on the brink of tears.

By the time I finished with my thoughts, we were pulling up to the warehouse. I noticed Uncle V's car was already there and my ass got nervous as hell. This shit was about to be interesting and I was two seconds from bailing on this meeting. Besides, she didn't really need me here anyway. Walking inside, they were already talking and some bitch was all in Glitch's face. He laughed and I pulled my gun. Walking up to them, I cut that shit quick.

"Ha ha hell. Move around." The girl looked like she wanted to say something, but he pushed her away. "Who the fuck is she? You must didn't let her know I will push her shit back." Shrugging his shoulders, his ass tried to downplay it.

"I don't know, she came with Vicious and his boys. I was laughing about old stories. Calm down baby, you know ain't no other hoe out here for me but you." Turning my head as fast as I could, I was ready to slap his ass.

"Excuse me."

"Baby don't try to act like I didn't get a used car with miles on it. It's all good though because I like vintage." Smacking him in the head, I tried to stand behind him so Vicious couldn't see me.

"Boo, you don't have to hide. We'll talk later. Right now, we are here to solve a problem. Me and my crew will help you with whatever you need. Roulette, you're up." Rolling her eyes, she addressed the room. This was going to be a mess.

This was a power struggle I really wish I didn't have to be a part of. These two were frick and frack. One in the same and they didn't know it. Instead of both of them fighting for the number one spot, they would be a force to reckon with if they came together. They can bring the city to its knees if they joined forces, but knowing the both of them like I do, that shit wasn't gone happen. I'm going to try my best to stay out of this shit show, but at the end of the day, my loyalty is to Roulette. We came in this shit together and it's only fair that I ride with her til the end. Now, I would never tell him that shit to his face and I prayed it never came to that.

"Listen up, just so we are clear, this is my shit. My daddy is only here for moral support. I'm still the head bitch in charge and nothing has changed that." The look on Vicious face said different and I was starting to think this shit was about to get all bad.

Chapter Five

ROULETTE

*M*y daddy thought he was slick, low key starting this meeting while I wasn't here. His ass know they fear him and wasn't going to tell him to shut the fuck up. Whatever plan he told them to do, I knew they ass listened. The shit was going to get done, and I needed to figure out what the fuck it was. If he was going to go behind me, I will cut him out of my meetings. Whether he liked it or not, I was in charge.

"Now, is there anybody here who feels like Vicious is running shit?" The lil bitch that we didn't know raised her hand and came forward.

"With all due respect, there is only one Vicious. Yes, you are his daughter, but I mean for real. This is Vicious we are talking about. Are we really ready to be led by a mini me? We can have the real thing." Laughing, I walked over to my cabinet and grabbed my gun. I could see Breezy shaking her head telling me not to do it, but this shit was about to stop right here and now. Even though I was in front of her, I looked my daddy in his eyes as if it was him.

"Are you feeling lucky?" She looked confused.

"Excuse me?" Spinning the chamber, I continued to look at Vicious.

"I said, are you feeling lucky? Do you know how I got my name?" She looked at me like bitch no, so I explained it. "Well, when you're at my mercy, I give you the chance to beat the odds. I'll only pull the trigger twice playing a game of chance. Hence the name Roulette. Now, I ask you again, are you feeling lucky?" Turning towards Vicious, she looked to him for support.

"V."

"Don't look at him, look at me. I'm in charge, but it doesn't matter. Your time is up." Pulling the trigger, her brains exploded over Glitch.

"I guess she was able to give you some head after all." I laughed at Breezy until I saw my daddy's face.

"You lucky I just recruited her or you would have written a check your ass couldn't cash. Carry on with the fucking meeting."

"Like I said, I'm in charge. Does anybody else have a problem with that?" No one spoke up, but I could see my daddy's jaw clenching. I was about to talk when my phone rang. It was unknown, but I decided to answer.

"How do yall feel about your boss taking a call in the middle of a meeting? That shit tacky." Vicious and his crew laughed, but I didn't find shit funny. I knew he was only talking shit, but he was causing a rift in my camp. Ignoring his ass, I took my call. Once I hung up, I turned to everyone there.

"Okay, I was just informed that Capone didn't die. I'm going to go finish what I started while I can. My daddy always said, if you cut off the head, the body will fall. If it's a war they want, that's what the fuck they are going to get."

"Me and Glitch will go with you." Breezy was ready to ride, but I wasn't allowing it this time.

"He is asking for me because he has questions. If I come in there with my crew, I'll never get past his security. I'm not the boss for shit. I got this." Out of all that shit my daddy talked, he now looked concerned.

"Baby girl, if you need me, I got you. Make daddy proud." Laughing, I headed out towards the hospital. On the outside, I was keeping it together. On the inside though, I was going crazy. This was the man that I loved and I thought I was going to be with, but his ass was a snake ass bitch that was seeking revenge. Jumping in the car, I drove towards the hospital with mad thoughts on my mind. What made Shitz call me? Was this a set up? I shot this nigga up, but he was asking for me to come to the hospital. Knowing I didn't have time for all of that, I needed to clear my head and prepare for what was to come.

Getting out of my car, I walked inside and headed upstairs. I know I supposed to get a visitor's pass, but I didn't want a record of me being here. Heading to the room that Shitz gave me, I froze seeing his mother at the bed. It looked as if she was trying to smother him. That shit didn't make sense and it had my mind racing. Why would she be trying to kill him? Knowing that I now needed answers, I had to leave him alive for a lil while. Stepping forward, I decided to let my presence be known to see how she would react. I could be reading this wrong.

"Hey, how is he?" I know that was a dumb question since I was the one that put him there, but I wanted to see her reaction. The bitch jumped and started adjusting his pillow behind his head.

"He is fine, no thanks to you. I don't know why he wants to see you, but I am going to leave and let you all talk. Oh, how is Vicious? Tell him I said hello will you." This bitch thought she was slick, but I know she was just in here trying to kill him.

"He's fine, you want me to give him a message?"

"Just tell him Rebecca says hello." Nodding my head, I kept my hand close to my gun until she walked out. Something was off and I need to find out what the fuck is wrong with this picture. As soon as I was sure that she was gone, I walked over to his bed. His ass was knocked out and it would be nothing to kill him, but I needed answers. If him and his mama was plotting revenge against us, why the fuck would she be trying to kill him? I was still alive and there was no reason to take him out. Sitting down in the chair, I pulled my phone out and called my daddy. I needed him to know my decision to keep Capone alive for now. Picking up on the first ring, you could tell he was happy to hear I was okay.

"Hey daddy. Change of plans. When I got here his mama was trying to kill him and that shit doesn't make sense at all. I need answers and only he can give them to me."

"The shit definitely don't make sense. I'm not sure what the fuck is going on, but you're doing the right thing. Once you get your answers, you know what you have to do."

"I know and the bitch asked about you. Said to tell you Rebecca said hi. Stuck up bitch pissed me off, but I had to make her think shit was cool."

"That's who his mother is? Shit keep getting deeper. Rebecca is the girl that Vega made me fuck that night. I knew his ass was on some shady shit, that's why I didn't give a fuck about taking his ass out. You did good grasshopper. Now finish the rest and call a meeting when you're done."

"Didn't I tell your old ass I'm in charge? I'm going to finish the rest and I'll call a meeting when I'm done." Laughing, we both hung up the phone.

"So, you only came to finish the job?" Hearing Capone's voice sent chills down my spine. I wonder how much he heard. Walking over to the bed, he turned to look at me. I don't know why my pussy was begging me to sit on top of him when I needed to be putting a bullet in his head.

"I came for answers."

"That's funny, because I called you here for the same thing. Why did you try to kill me?" His ass was still trying to play slow and it was pissing me off.

"After I left your house I went to tell my daddy about us, and I got the surprise of my life. Twenty two years ago, my daddy made a deal with yours and because of him being there, my mama died. He blamed your father and went back to kill him. You were there when he did it. Now, you're after me for revenge. What I don't understand is, if you and your mama is working together to take us out, why would she be in here trying to kill you? Did you cross her too?" The look on his face told me everything I needed to know. His ass didn't know what the fuck I was talking about.

"My mother told me and everyone else, that my dad was killed in a robbery. No one knew who it was or what they took. He went out the way he lived and in our world it's honorable. No one ever had any reason to question that. I had no idea your father killed mine, but now I know why my mama was pushing so hard for us to be together. She has to know. I don't know why she was in here trying to kill me and I don't even know if I believe you." If he wasn't already injured, I would have slapped his ass back to sleep.

"I have no reason to lie to you. When I walked in here, she was smothering your ass. I don't know what the fuck is going on, but the shit ain't adding up." He actually laughed.

"It makes perfect sense. If my mama knows your dad killed mine, she is the one that has been after you. Each time I mentioned that we back you up and Vicious wasn't our responsibility, she would say that it was out of my league and she would handle him. I thought she was just talking shit. If you say she tried to kill me, I'm just as lost as you. Shitz said she hadn't been here since I was admitted and that was a week ago." This shit was freaky, but I knew what I had to do.

"I know you probably don't trust me right now, but you need to. My camp is waiting for me to give them the word that you are dead. Your mama is trying to kill you and right now, we need to figure out why. Until then, I need to hide you from everybody. To the world, you need to be dead."

"Do what you need to do."

"First, I have to find someone I can pay off. They need to give you a death certificate and you need to write up a letter making me your power of attorney. I have to cremate you so there is no body. In order for them to stop looking, this is the way that we have to do this. I need to go set some stuff up for a place to hide you. Don't take any more pain meds, your ass need to be coherent just in case your mama come back. I'll be gone a few hours. Right now, don't trust anyone but me. No matter what they tell you. I won't send anyone up here to check on you, so don't fall for it. We good?"

"Yea we good. Hurry the fuck up, I don't trust anyone at this point. Not even you, but we both searching for answers. I don't want to be here long enough for them to come, so get moving." Walking out of his room, I knew this was going to be bad. My daddy would consider this a betrayal and so would my crew. This may be the end of Roulette, and now I was making myself a target.

Chapter Six

VICIOUS

*T*he crew was looking for answers, mine and Kalina's included. I was trying not to take charge, but her ass been gone for hours and no one had heard anything. The savage in me wanted to just bark out orders, but the father in me was nervous as fuck.

"You all are looking for something to do, and we all are ready to get our hands dirty. I know that, but the only thing I need is for you mother fuckers to find my daughter. It's been three hours, and if it hits four, some heads are going to spin. You have never seen me at my worst, but you will in forty nine minutes. FIND HER NOW!!!" Everybody started shuffling around trying to figure out what to do or where to start.

"Is everyone here? Let's get down to business please." Kalina walked her ass in here like she wasn't missing for hours and thought she wasn't gone explain what the fuck happened.

"Kalina where were you?" Turning to me, she shot daggers my way.

"In here, I'm Roulette. If you calm down long enough, you will know where I was."

"Just tell us what the fuck happened. Did you finish the job?"

"After talking to you, I waited for him to wake up. When he did I was questioning him and his ass started to crash. They put me out the room and rushed him to surgery. I waited for him for hours. They came out and told me he died in surgery. I didn't have to kill him, he is no longer a threat. From the little bit that I got out of him, his mama is behind the shit and we need to find out what she has planned." I tried to let her do things her way and I no longer wanted to fight with my daughter.

"Okay good. I'm sure you will put your ears to the street and me and mine will do the same. Good job baby girl." Watching her smile at me because I gave my approval, let me know I did the right thing.

"Alright, I'll keep you updated on everything I find out. You heard what we said, get to work people. Bring me back something useful and bring it fast." Her crew flew out of there fast and I was proud at how loyal they were to her. Boo, Kalina, and Glitch walked out together and it left me and my crew. When I turned to them, Grew started laughing.

"Let me guess, that's not what we are doing?" Shaking my head, I sighed with frustration.

"No. She wants answers and I don't give a fuck about the reasoning. We know who is after us, I know who killed Fat Back, and they don't get to sleep another night in my city. Let's go." Piling in my truck, we headed towards the Vega compound. This shit felt familiar as hell. Getting in go mode, I zoned out as much as I could since I was driving.

When we pulled up, I had a strange feeling of déjà vu. I've done this dance twenty two years ago and I was ready to put an end to this shit. As soon as I parked, I looked over to my crew. It was the three of us last time and we barely made it out with our lives. Vicious will always come out on top, but I don't want to lose none of my team. They been rocking with me since the beginning and I'm just as responsible for them as I was Fat Back. These were my niggas and I had to make sure this is what they were ready for. Hell, we were older and they may not want to go to war again.

"Ok ladies."

"Fuck you." They both screamed that out and I laughed.

"For real, listen up. I know yall rocking until the wheels fall off and I appreciate yall for that shit. I know this is not what you were signing up for and I get that. If you want to walk away, I won't feel a way. We've grown older and you got shit going on. Last chance to walk away before we go in here into the unknown." They looked at me and I could see doubt in their eyes. It's been a long time since they been in this rodeo. They were old and doubting their skills. Me, I snuck out often and did a kill just to satisfy the thirst. From the looks on their faces, I know they haven't done the same.

"Vicious, you know where our loyalty lies. We been at this shit a long time and we've never turned our backs on you. With that being said, you know I got a shaky hand and it has gotten worse with old age, but I got you. Just don't let these bitch ass niggas sneak up behind me." Grew was gone always ride, but I often worried about that pissy ass hand. Nigga fuck around and shoot me like Arsenio shot Junior.

"You know I got you. I'm not as fast as I used to be, but I can still shoot this mother fucker. Hell, my nuts stopped putting out babies a long time ago, but I still be shooting them bitches."

"My niggas. Let's get it then. Stay alert and watch each other's back. You know the drill." Getting out the car, we headed through the gate with no problems. It was open and that made me go on instant alert.

Heading inside, there was no sight of security. Either they haven't had time to recoup or they ass were staying out of the open. Walking through each room, we searched every door and opened each hidden wall. We been here before and I knew of a few. Only because Vega's men were trying to get the fuck out of there.

"What the fuck. Either these niggas hiding like the good roaches that stay away when company comes over, or this shit a ghost town." E Way was right. Something was off.

Walking through a few more rooms, we did the same thing and didn't find anyone. Shit was weird and I wasn't liking this feeling.

Making sure I covered my niggas, we continued to walk through the rest of the house.

"Aight listen, I know we all are feeling like some shit off in this bitch and maybe that's what they want us to feel. It's one more section to the house and that's Vega's section as we already know. We can walk into that wing and they try to light our ass up or we can go in there and it's empty as well. All I'm saying is be prepared for anything. I'll walk in first, E Way take the end."

Easing up the stairs, we walked slowly and quietly. The silence was about to drive me crazy and I was ready to shoot just to make some noise. Shit was driving me crazy, but I was at the door now. Opening it, I headed inside. Looking around, I fell out laughing. It was nobody in here. My ass thought they were about to do a sneak attack, but they ass was gone.

"I guess these niggas got gone because they knew that we were coming. These bitches ran." That's why I really didn't want Kalina running the city. Women thought differently. Niggas didn't run. If it was me, we would have been waiting guns drawn. It would have been one hell of a shoot out and my men would have been the last ones standing.

Instead, here we were looking at each other like some damn dummies. How the fuck was Rebecca in charge of everything. There was no way Vega would have let her fuck other niggas if she was his everything. He used her ass like a pawn and had something up his sleeve. I don't know what, but I can feel it now like I did twenty two years ago.

Not only was she in charge, she wanted me to know that she was. Rebecca was around, she heard the stories and she knew who I was. If a nigga sent for me, I was coming. I'm sure she knew I put the shit together about Fat Back. The bitch wanted me to know that she was the one behind it. So why run? Why the fuck would you have me to come out here only to disappear like some fucking bitches.

Looking around the room, I tried to piece the shit together. I've been out the game for a while and it was taking me a little longer.

Back in the days, it would have come to me right away. I was missing something and then it hit me. The bitch wanted me here because she knew I would come. They wanted to take us out, just not the way that we thought.

"The compound is about to blow up."

Chapter Seven

BREEZY

*S*itting in the car, I wanted to address the elephant in the room, but everyone else was trying to ignore it. Roulette has been my best friend since before we could talk. I know her like I know myself and she was hiding something. Her ass don't look the least bit heart broken, but she just told us her nigga died and there is no emotion going through her.

"I'll meet up with yall later. I got some shit to handle and I need to head out. Breezy, I hope your lazy ass cooking tonight, a nigga gone be hungry as fuck when I get back." Leaning in, I kissed him.

"I got you." When he got out, my ass went the fuck off.

"This nigga thinks I'm stupid. Either he cheating on me or his bitch ass working for the other side. I'll beat that nigga with his extra meat if he thinks he is going to cheat on me." Crying, all I could do was break down. "Roulette, what if he working for the other side?"

"Friend, why the fuck would you say some shit like that? Glitch been one hundred since he's known us. No matter who came and left, it has always been us."

"Bitch you mean when your ass killed them all but think about it. Every time we're in a meeting, he heads out. When I got shot up, he was conveniently out of town. Shit not adding up, so if he is not a traitor, his ass is cheating." I knew I was right on the money because Roulette gave me a sympathetic look.

"I'm sorry best friend. You know how this story ends and I know how you feel about him. If what you are saying is true, we gotta take him out. Glitch is my right hand, so I need you to be sure. Friend are you sure?"

"Bitch were you sure when your dick was setting your ass up? Of course I'm not sure. This nigga been acting like everything was normal when he come home. Fucking me with that lil tuck tuck and shit."

"This nigga better not be around here lying and shit." Looking at her, I thought about what I needed to say to her ass. She was over here judging me and tuck dick, but she had some explaining to do.

"Speaking of lying, bitch you know damn well I know your ass better than you know yourself. If that nigga was dead, you would have broken down by now. I don't know what is going on, but you better tell me something before I call and tell your daddy.

"I wish you would. I'm going to start calling your ass snitch bitch."

"Spill it hoe before I slap you with my left tittie. You know that bitch longer than my right one, it can reach." Looking at her sigh, I started to tell her never mind. It sounded like something big and my ass was just too nosy to not hear it. Eating some imaginary popcorn while I sipped my tea, I waited for her to give me the juicy shit.

"Okay, so I kind of lied about it all. He had no idea that my daddy killed his. His mama was in there trying to kill him when I walked in and the bitch just seemed off to me. After talking, the only logical thing to do was move him. Bitch it took me that long because I had to pay someone to fake his death and get him the fuck out of there before Vicious or his mama took his life." My ass wanted to jump out of the car and run. I wanted the tea but this bitch just served me a shot of Hennessy.

"No bitch. Noooo. You need to run and go hide wherever the fuck you put that nigga. We don't know if he is playing you or what. You know like I do, the right thing to do was take him out. We don't leave room for doubt. On top of that, bitch you crossed the crew.

That's a war within itself and now you done dragged my ass into it. Nope bitch, throw down the anchor my ass getting the fuck off this sinking ship."

"Calm your ass down. I have it all under control. Until we can figure out what his mama is up to, I will keep him hidden away. If he is not a traitor, then no harm no foul. If the nigga flaw, I can take him out and he will really be dead." This girl has lost her mind. She was not getting it. Vicious was like a damn hound, he found out everything.

"You know I have your back, but I'm telling you now as your friend, this is the wrong call. You just put me in some shit I didn't want to be in. Your dad is going to find out, you know how he is. God help us all."

"You so damn dramatic. As long as you keep your mouth shut, especially to Glitch, we will be good. No one will know, I promise. We just have to find out what the fuck his mama is up to.

"You spitting a lot of we around here. Bitch the only French I know is fries. I'll keep your secret, but if Uncle V comes to me, I'm telling on your ass and when did your ass become so damn slow?" I knew she wouldn't have the slightest idea of what I was talking about. My girl was in love and done fell off.

"What now?"

"You know your father. We've never seen him in action, but we heard the stories. There is no way your dad is standing around waiting for information. They ass somewhere kicking off a war with your dick's mama. He just told us what we wanted to hear. Him and his crew left together, where you thought they were going to an AARP meeting?" She was about to deny it and thought about it.

"Bitch we about to go crash some shit. He got me fucked up. If they ass was gone be in a shoot out, I will be leading the fucking pack." I wasn't as pumped as she was, but it would be interesting to see how it played out. This was going to be a war within itself. My ass was ready to get there, but Roulette was driving like she was crazy. I wanted a front row seat, but not in front of the Lord.

"Hey bestie, you think you can slow down?" Giving a nervous laugh, I looked at her waiting to see if she would slow down.

"I got this bitch. You know how many times I had to beat my daddy home. I've put this car on two wheels to make it back to that tunnel. If you're scared, put your seatbelt on."

"Bitch don't play me like I'm a fucking coward." I was talking shit, but I slid that seatbelt on right quick. I know Bugatti's are meant to drive fast, but this bitch was hitting corners like the girl that didn't make it on the fast and furious. As soon as we pulled up, we got out of the car. The grounds seemed quiet as hell, and I was concerned. Uncle V's car was here so we should be hearing gun shots. Instead, all I heard was Roulette breathing. When she opened the trunk, my pussy jumped a little. It was an entire arsenal in that bitch.

"You ready best friend?" Grabbing a shot gun, I nodded.

"Fuck yea I am." Walking towards the gate, we screamed as the compound blew up in front of us.

Chapter Eight

REBECCA

*O*h, have the tables have turned. I was having a damn good time watching everyone trying to figure out what was going on. No one knew what I was up to and I loved it that way. See, the thing is, Vicious ass was too cocky. He thought the sins of his past went away because his ass disappeared for twenty two years. That was not the case.

I've been waiting on his return for a long time. I knew that one day, he would resurface. Men like that just can't walk away for good. His ass was in the background lurking and I knew that something was going to bring him out. If I had known it would be his daughter, I would have went that route a long time ago.

From the moment she walked into our office, I knew it was some kind of relation. She looked just like him. When Capone confirmed it, I knew I had his ass. See, all that time, I wanted to kill him and leave it at that. This plan was much better. I could tear his daughter to shreds and take all his money. Well, at least that's what I thought I was going to do. My incompetent ass son couldn't even do his part. That lil bitch was running amuck and his ass couldn't do shit about it. He was nothing like his father, but in that way, he was. She walked all over his simple ass and I had to stand by and watch the shit hoping it was for a good cause.

My son didn't know, I had cameras installed everywhere and I knew whatever went on in my house. The only time I turned away is when they ass was having sex. I just knew he was going to use his meat to get what he wanted out of her, but his ass couldn't do that. His father used that lil ass dick of his to get what he wanted, so I thought his ass could too. My mistake.

Not only did this nigga allow this lil bitch to treat him like shit, he stood his dumb ass there while she shot him up. Security tried to handle her and he let her go. There is no room for something like that on my team. He liked to believe that he was in charge, but he had no idea the lengths I have gone through. I was the devil himself and my son had no idea.

His ass thought he was running shit, and I liked to let him think he was. There is nothing that he did that I didn't give the okay or shut it down. Him and his dumb ass friend Shitz thought they were some boss ass niggas, when all they were was some errand boys. Doing my dirty work. Every deal they made, it was me that made it happen. By the time they called in, I had already sealed the deal.

There was no way I was allowing another Vega man to run me or my household. This shit was going to be done the way that I saw fit and that's how the shit was going to stay. The lil bitch walked in on me about to take his weak ass out and I didn't need that. Hopefully, she was there to do the same thing. My phone ringing brought me out of my thoughts.

"Mrs. Vega how can I help you?" It was an unknown number and I had no idea who was on the other end of the phone. I hope it was Vicious calling to meet up.

"This is Dr. Granger at Advocate South Hospital. We would like for you to come up here so we can talk to you about your son. Are you available to come in?" I wanted to tell they ass hell naw, let him die but I couldn't.

"I'm on the way." Calling my driver, I headed towards the hospital to see what the weak ass punk needed. If his ass needed a donor, that nigga was assed out. Pulling up, I put my game face on so I could pretend to be mother of the year. Walking inside, I went into pissed mother mode.

"Excuse me. Who is in charge? I need to speak to someone about my son and someone better approach this desk right now or I will shut this hospital down." Some young ass nurse came running towards me and I wanted to slap her with my gloves. If they hadn't cost a thousand dollars, I probably would have.

"I'm sorry ma'am. How can I help you?"

"You can page Dr. Granger thank you." Rolling my eyes, I walked away. There was no way she would get anything more out of me.

"Hell Mrs. Vega, I'm Dr. Granger and maybe you should sit down."

"Maybe you should do your job and tell me why I'm here. If I wanted to sit down, I know how to bend my legs." He looked as if he was trying to avoid saying something disrespectful.

"Well, getting straight to the point. Your son passed away a few hours ago. I wanted to know if you wanted to know where to pick up his remains?" Now my ass was confused.

"You're just now telling me that my son died. So who in the fuck ordered him to be cremated?" You could tell he was uncomfortable with this line of questioning.

"A Mrs. Kalina Barnes. He had her down as his power of attorney. When he passed away, she ordered him to be cremated and then left." It took everything in me not to laugh.

"Write down where this funeral home is and I will go and pick it up." Once he gave me the paper, I faked a cry and got my ass up out of there. Grabbing my phone as I got in the car, I called Shitz.

"What's up Mrs. V?"

"Did you know that Capone passed away? The lil bitch killed him and then had his ass cremated. His dumb ass had her on his paper work. What kind of idiot of a son did I raise?" The phone went silent and then he started talking.

"I don't know shit about that. I told his ass let me take her out, but he wanted to talk to her. I knew I shouldn't have called her ass up there."

"Everybody can't be as smart as me. Tomorrow you are going to go pick up his dusty ass remains."

"Say less." Hanging up the phone, I laid back and closed my eyes. Out of nowhere, I shot my ass back up. If I didn't know shit else, I knew bullshit. She wasn't there to kill him, my son asked for her. All of a sudden, she is his power of attorney and had him cremated. These niggas thought they could pull one over on me. This could only mean one thing, they were coming after me and my son helped them do it. Grabbing my phone, I called my security.

"Get everyone out of the house. Leave the gate open and make sure that no one stays behind."

"Are you sure boss lady, I can make sure everything is straight."

"Just do what the fuck I asked you and hurry up. If you're there in ten minutes, that shit on your ass." Hanging up, I smiled. I had a trick for all of them. This was about to be an explosive ass twist, I hope they ass was ready for it.

Chapter Nine

CAPONE

*S*hit was out of control and I had no idea what was going on. One thing I knew, I couldn't figure the shit out hid away in this damn house. Roulette hadn't come back and it's been a month. She made sure I had a great nursing staff, but I was going crazy wondering what was happening. Finishing up my therapy, I headed to the shower. It felt good to be able to walk. At least I didn't have to lay around all damn day while I tried to piece this shit together.

Once I was done taking care of my hygiene, I wrapped my towel and walked out of the bathroom. Roulette was standing there listening to the nurse and therapist update her on how I was doing. She finally turned to look at me and I had to turn around to keep her from seeing my dick. The shit was rising and I knew we weren't there.

"Hey, they told me you're doing great. How are you feeling?" I'm feeling like I want you to put your mouth on my dick. How do you think I'm feeling? I would be feeling so much better if you just let me stick the tip in.

"I'm good. Tired of being in the house left in the dark. What's going on Roulette?" Motioning for the staff to leave the room, shorty started giving me an update.

"Your mother blew your compound up while my father and his crew were inside." Grabbing her, I held her close. Here I was thinking about sticking my dick in her and her father died. Our parents killed each other.

"I'm sorry shorty." Pulling back, she started laughing.

"I'm sorry if you misunderstood. He didn't die, apparently they got out of there before it happened. They are looking for her and I'm sorry, but I need you to tell me where she could be hiding." She asked me that shit like it was nothing. Even though the bitch tried to kill me, she was still my mother and I needed to know why. If anyone was going to kill her, it would be me.

"I'll handle that myself. Tell your daddy to stand down." From the look on her face, I could tell we were about to have it out.

"Capone, I'm trying to believe that you had nothing to do with this plan but you are making it hard. I'm not asking you to give me an address, I'm telling you to. You think this shit is all laughs and giggles. This shit ain't a fucking game. Did you not get my message when I shot you the first fucking time?" Walking close to her, I leaned in.

"Maybe you didn't get the message the first time. You don't run me. I'm that nigga and I don't take orders from a mother fucking soul. You keep trying to flex on me shorty like I'm some soft ass nigga. If that's what you looking for, I'll drive you through boys town. They got a lot of soft dicks. Want one?" Slapping me in my face, she was ready to fight.

"Fuck you." Slamming her on the bed, I climbed on top of her.

"What did I tell you last time? If you put your hands on me, you will pay one way or another." Taking my leg, I pushed her legs apart forcefully. Even though I was in pain, I refused to let her know that. Snatching her leggings down, I ran my fingers up her slit. It's like she was paralyzed. Shorty wouldn't talk or move but that shit was about to change. Pushing my dick inside of her, I needed to feel her on me before I punished her ass. The way she gasped, I knew she was missing me as much as I missed her. Pulling out, I flipped her over and took charge.

I know I shouldn't be having aggressive sex, but I was tired of her thinking shit was sweet. Snatching her body towards me, I forced her on her legs. She had no idea how I was about to fuck her up, but that's what was about to happen. Spitting on her ass, I pushed my dick inside before she realized what happened.

"Oww what the fuck. Capone no. Pull out please, this shit hurts so bad. Fuck. You're ripping my ass."

"What the fuck I tell you about putting your hands on me? Are you going to stop putting your fucking hands on me?"

"Yes, please take this big ass dick out of my ass. I think my colon done fell out. CHECK THE MATRESS FOR MY DAMN COLON." It took everything in me not to fall the fuck out laughing. Reaching under her, I started playing with her pussy.

"You gone take this dick until you learn to keep your fucking hands to yourself." After stroking her pussy for five minutes while I dropped this dick in her ass, she squirted everywhere.

"See, your ass done knocked out my damn bladder. If you don't take this damn donkey dick out of my ass, I'm going to fuck you up. Okay, okay. I get it. I'm sorry. I won't hit you anymore. You won, I promise I'll keep my hands to myself donkey kong. I don't' wanna lose my ass." Laughing, I knew she had learned her lesson. And she came whether she knew it or not. Pulling my dick out, she collapsed on the bed. Walking to the bathroom, I washed my dick off. When I walked back in the room, shorty was lying in the bed snoring like a damn bear. Slapping her on the ass, I woke her up.

"I still need to nut, wake your ass up." When she fell back out and started snoring, I left her ass alone. Hopefully this wouldn't be the last time, but I wasn't against taking that shit. Once she got something in her head, she ran with that shit.

Just because she had sex with me didn't mean shit. Her ass will do a drive by on my ass in a minute. I've never had a chick fuck the shit out of me, then leave me sitting there feeling lonely and lost. This girl had a way of playing on my emotions and I had no idea when she would pull that shit. It took her a month to come back this time, ain't no telling how long it will be before she come back the next time.

"Oh my God, I just shitted on myself. I'm about to fuck you up. You took my booty hole. How the fuck am I gone walk around with loose booty. I hate you so much right now. The donkey made me lose my booty hole." When she started crying, I knew her ass wasn't coming back no time soon. My petty ass fucked up.

Chapter Ten

ROULETTE

*L*ying in the bed with asshole on my chin, I wanted to beat the shit out of Capone. No matter how upset I was, I needed to keep my hands to myself. His petty was on a different level and I couldn't take that shit no more. He won, I don't know how Breezy can do this shit out of pleasure. It was the worst thing I ever felt in my life. Trying my best to roll over, I looked to him for answers.

"I know that this is hard because it's your mama, but we have to find her and put an end to that shit. You know if we don't, then my family is in jeopardy. I, am in jeopardy." The perplexed look on his face told me he wouldn't make the right decision.

"Look, I'm not disputing that. All I'm saying is, that she is my mama and I should be the one to handle her. I can't do that as long as you want me hidden away. I need to be out there in the streets, that's who I am."

"Listen, I know that you're tired of being here. You have to, no I need you to understand what will happen. You have people from both sides that will kill you. My daddy, will kill you. I'm not saying you can't handle yourself, I just don't want to lose you. I need the chance to fix this." His jaw line clenched, but he smiled.

"You didn't break anything, and I don't need you fixing it for me. I'm not as weak as you think I am. I'll give you one month. If you don't have this shit done by then, I'll handle it on my own. Now get your ass up and get to work. The clock is ticking." Getting up out of the bed, I had to hold back tears. My ass felt like it was splitting. After handling my hygiene the best way I could, I got dressed and tip toed my way out of the house. A bitch could barely walk and I was pissed at myself. It felt like my left ass cheek was numb and I could shit at any moment.

Heading to Breezy's house, I cried the entire way there. I need a pillow to put under my ass or this shit wasn't gone work. How the fuck was I gone find this loony bitch if I couldn't walk? Pulling up to Breezy's house, I put the code in and parked. As soon as I got out, I heard shit breaking and I had no idea what the fuck was going on. I know this bitch is not here trying to kill my friend. Grabbing my Desert Eagle, I tried to run but that shit wasn't working. Donkey dick had my ass out here waddling and in this moment, I hated him.

Walking like a bitch was trying to hit the quan, I finally made it inside. You could hear glass breaking and someone screaming. Listening closely, I knew it was Breezy. Fuck. Tipping through the house, I made my way to the room where she was. Raising my gun, I rounded the corner ready to lay a nigga out. What I saw fucked me up. Glitch was tied up to a chair and she had his mouth taped shut. Breezy was standing over him throwing dishes and vases at his ass. He couldn't do shit but take it.

"You think I'm playing with you? If you don't tell me where the fuck you have been, I will beat your ass to death." I looked at her like she was crazy.

"Umm excuse me. How can he tell you when you have his mouth taped and you beating him with plates?" Realizing I was in the room, I thought she would stop. Instead, she kept on with her line of questioning. Grabbing a pot, she hit his ass over the head with it.

"Nigga where the fuck you been?" Even though Glitch may be suspect, I felt bad for him.

"Bestie, let him go. This nigga is going to kill you when he gets free. Let him go while you still can." When she grabbed the skillet, I knew she was at a point of no return.

"I'm not stopping until I have used every pot in the kitchen. He wants to sling that lil meat around, he can swing it in one of these pots. Don't get quiet on me now mother fucker. Where your big balls at now." Refusing to watch her talk to herself and beat this nigga, I left her with that shit. Heading to the warehouse, I needed to see if the crew had any information.

Jumping in my Camaro, I headed to the city. Boyz In the Hood was playing, but my mind was on my ass. I had to concentrate on not putting too much pressure and the shit is harder than people think. Pulling up, I tip toed inside and found my dad and his crew there to my surprise. What pissed me off the most, was the fact that my crew was there as well. This nigga was trying to take charge behind my back. They didn't hear me coming since my ass had to tip toe.

"This is interesting. I don't recall asking you to come in." My dad was looking at how I was walking, but I ignored him.

"We were here waiting further instructions from you. Been here since yesterday. Where exactly were you again?" Not about to go into that, I ignored that as well.

"If you sat your dumb ass in a warehouse when no meeting was called, then that's on you. Now, here is what you all can do. Find Rebecca. She has not left. I'm sure she is somewhere lurking."

"Don't get your ass slapped up. Grew and E Way, go with these young niggas and teach them a thing or two. Ka, I mean Roulette, come with me. We'll meet up in a few hours to give an update." I wanted to slap him for taking charge and delegating how I should have, but my ass was itching and I was concentrating on not scratching. Walking out the door, he headed towards his car and I went to mine. You could see the aggravation on his face. He wanted me to follow his lead.

"Baby girl, it is easier if we take my truck. Let's go, you're wasting time."

"Nigga if you don't get your ass in this car. Did you see how I was walking? I wish I would walk my ass back over there." Grunting, he came and got in my car. Throwing my shades on, I smiled knowing I won this round. He tried to sneak me behind my back with the team, but at the end of the day, he had to listen to me. If I told my crew to take him out, they had to because I was in charge. His ass needed to learn he was a thing of the past.

"Listen, when we get out there in these streets, you have to let me take the lead. They fear me more and I can get more out of them than you can." Looking over to him, I laughed.

"All you need to worry about is if you have enough velvet boxes in that bag of yours. I've been doing this for a while now. I was out here in these same streets while you were at home eating oatmeal and watching the soaps. You're a legend, you should allow yourself to go out on top. Don't kill out your legacy trying to prove a point, but you're not the same. Your ass is old and you need to accept it." I didn't believe none of the shit I said, but I wanted to fuck with him since he went behind my back. It was an honor to be out here with my dad in these streets, but I meant what I said on one thing. I was in charge and his old ass was gone have to step back and accept it.

"I'm about to show your ass old. You heard the stories, but you about to see it first hand. I got guns older than your ass." Turning up the radio, I laughed on the inside.

Chapter Eleven

VICIOUS

Kalina don't know how deep her words cut me. Probably because I was struggling with those same thoughts. If it wasn't for that bitch killing Fat Back, I would have never come out of retirement. I didn't have time to doubt myself about that, I acted on instinct and emotion. Now, my dumb ass done made her come with me trying to teach her a lesson and she had me doubting myself.

If she wasn't my daughter, I would shoot the fuck out of her ass for making me think this way. Shaking that shit off, I knew I had to get it together. I was Vicious, that shit ran through my blood and no amount of time off was going to change that. If Kalina wanted to see who I was, she was in for one hell of a show. As soon as we pulled up to one of the Vega's spots, I jumped out and shot the security that was on the porch. One shot, one swift motion, no remorse. Her ass was struggling to get out of the car and I laughed at her expense. I have no idea what was going on with her, but I used it to my advantage. By the time she caught up, I would be in Vicious mode. Walking inside, everyone looked around at me like what the fuck.

"One person gets to live. The first one to start talking is the lucky mother fucker. Now, who is it gonna be?" You could tell they were trying to figure out if I was serious or not. Raising my gun, I shot the guy closest to me. Everyone raised their guns and I smiled. "I don't think you want to do that. It would be smart for one of you to work with me or all of you die." I'm guessing the one in charge decided to speak up.

"Why the fuck you coming up in our shit barking orders? Who the fuck you think you are? This our shit and you the one that's about to have a long night." Right as I was thinking where the hell was Kalina, she walked in behind them guns drawn.

"He's Vicious? You haven't heard that he was back, well I don't even have to ask my question. You're definitely lucky. You get to witness a legend in person." The looks on their faces changed immediately. It went from cocky, to fear. In that moment, I knew I still had it. Even if I didn't, my name alone kept me in the game.

"Vicious, I was a kid when you were terrorizing these streets. I don't know why you are here, but we respect you. Whoever pissed you off, it wasn't us." Smiling, I stepped forward.

"Are you going to be the one to tell me what I want to know? See, we have a problem whether or not you know it's there. I'm only willing to leave one person alive, so tell me. Is that you?" His crew started to look nervous and I could tell he didn't want to make that call. Kalina fired five shots dropping all the men around him.

"Oh damn, I forgot. Are you feeling lucky? Guess not, carry on." Watching her tip toe over to her seat had me feeling like a proud father. They wasn't lying when they said she was just like me. I was about to do the same thing.

"Guess it's you. Now, if you tell me what I want to know, I'll let you live. You're right, it has nothing to do with you directly. I need to know where your boss is hiding. You have to meet up with someone." I knew he didn't really know where she was from the look on his face.

"If I knew, I would tell you. The only thing I know is they are picking up a shipment in two hours. We were about to go meet her when you barged in." After he told me where the pick up was, I slammed him to the ground. You can tell he was confused.

"I told you everything I know." Kicking him in the mouth, he screamed out in pain. As soon as he did, I pulled my knife and jumped on top of him. Before he could realize what was happening, I had his tongue in my hand. One swift motion, his tongue was unattached. Not wanting him to be in pain long, I slit his throat and stood up.

"Damn, I didn't realize you did the shit so fast and easy. I always thought it was a long drawn out thing. The legendary Vicious does have heart. Good job old man, now help me up." Laughing, I walked over to her and pulled her up.

"Baby girl, ain't shit old about me but my money. What you just saw was perfection. You won't admit it now, but you were impressed as hell. I bet you wish you could do that shit. What happened to your ass, why the fuck you walking like that?"

"Mind your damn business. When this is over, you are going to teach me how to do that shit."

"If I teach you my signature, then there is no need for me. You just keep chucking your gun dirty harry. That's your signature." Laughing, she slapped me in the arm.

"Screw you." Pulling off, she headed towards the pickup location. We wanted to get there before anyone else so that we can scope out the scene. Hiding the car, we got out and found a secure location to wait. Thankfully, it was a lot of containers so we weren't exposed.

Two hours later, cars were pulling up. Either Rebecca was coming after them or she wasn't showing up at all. It was a bunch of men there, but no Rebecca. I hadn't seen her in years, but I'm sure she hadn't grown a beard and started wearing Tims. This bitch was playing games and she was starting to piss me off. Who the fuck kicks off a war and then hides. She was setting her men up to take the hit while she sat comfortably somewhere.

"The bitch not showing up, but we can damn sure send her a message. If we take enough of their ass out, she eventually will come out of hiding." Roulette nodded in agreement and we raised our guns. Walking towards the men, I thought about all that old man shit she was talking and decided to be petty. Pushing her forward, I stuck my feet out and she went crashing to the ground. Knowing she couldn't walk fast, I ran towards the men.

Without worrying about who will snitch, I raised my guns and took out all of the men except one. Watching those bodies drop gave me an adrenaline rush. Looking at the last man standing, he seemed to be frozen in place. Fear was good, he may just tell me everything. Before I could ask him anything, a bullet went through his head.

"Why the fuck would you kill the only person that could tell us anything?" Shrugging her shoulders, the mother fucker laughed. I could have killed her for the stunt she pulled. Now we wouldn't find Rebecca.

"You're the great almighty Vicious. You will find somebody else to tell you. Better hit those streets old man."

"I swear I should have put your ass up for adoption. You're an abomination to the Barnes name. I hope your ass is falling out." We both laughed and got in the car. All this time we been trying to out rank each other, when coming together was much more fun. I've never felt this with my crew. Seeing my baby girl in action had me proud as fuck. This could actually work.

Chapter Twelve

BREEZY

here's a stranger in my house. Took a while to figure out.
There's no way you could be who you say you are
You gotta be someone else.
Cus he wouldn't touch me like that
And he wouldn't treat me like you do

My ass talked all that shit to Roulette about sitting in the house being a bitch baby singing love songs, but my ass was in here belting out the lyrics to Stranger in My House by Tamia. I had no idea what the fuck was going on with Glitch, but I was over this shit. That nigga came in the house tired and wouldn't fuck me. After I begged him to, he tried to get away from me by going in another room.

I snuck up behind him and knocked that ass out. By the time he woke, I had been beating his ass for about ten minutes. I knew he couldn't answer me, but I wanted him to know I wasn't accepting no lies or bullshit when I let his ass go. I wanted the truth and I needed him to give it to me. At the time, it seemed like a great idea. It wasn't until I let him go that I thought, maybe, just maybe I may have fucked up. That nigga gave me a death look and I took off like a bat out of hell.

In my mind, all I had to do was make it up the stairs. If I could do that, I would lock his ass out and be safe. My ass was moving so fast, it seemed like my bunny slippers came to life. A bitch was moving out until he snatched me by my ankles and dragged me back down them bitches. When I say my tail bone had to be broken, I just knew there was no hope of me ever throwing this ass in a circle. I already couldn't dance, but now he killed all those chances.

When he flipped me over, my life flashed before my eyes. Seeing the blood running from his head and glass all over his clothes, I realized I may have gone too far. His chest was heaving up and down and I realized how sexy my boo was. I know I'm crazy, but he makes me like that. It's not that I didn't trust him, but he was making this shit hard as hell. Yea he had a lil extra meat, but bitches wanted his ass because he knew how to work that shit.

"If you wanted to fuck that's all the fuck you had to say. If you ever pull some shit like that again, you will lose me. Not for play, not for a lil while, but for good. I don't fight women, but I will beat a bitch's ass." Before I could respond, he was pushing his dick inside of me. The carpet was tearing my back up, but I was loving this shit. He knew me so well. All I needed was a lil meat and I would be good. All that disappearing and shit was making me paranoid. I didn't like that I was trying to figure out why my man keeps leaving and nobody knew where he was.

After rocking my world and my back against the stairs for an hour, he got up and left me lying there. When I made it up the stairs, he was in the shower. My dumb ass sat on the bed feeling bad as hell. I went too far this time, but that's who I was. I'm the crazy bust your windows and fuck you on the car type of girlfriend. I've always been that and it was a time he loved that about me. That only made my mind race more. A new woman was the only thing that could make him be tired of my bullshit. When he walked out, he grabbed his clothes to get dressed.

"Wait, where are you going?" The look of annoyance made me realize this stunt could make me lose him.

"I need a break. I've taken a lot of shit off you Breezy, but this was too much. If I have to fight killing you, I need to leave. This shit unhealthy and I can't do it. Just let me clear my head." I had a million things I wanted to say, but he didn't give me the chance. His ass walked out leaving me looking stupid. The tears came and I grabbed my phone. I needed to talk to Roulette.

"Hey best friend. Are you busy?" It sounded like she was out of breath and her ass better not be fucking and I was over here miserable.

"Naw, we just now finishing up. Me and daddy out here fucking shit up. We done killed so many people tonight I can barely breath from the adrenaline. All these years we could have been reigning supreme together, and I was scared to tell him. I'm glad he knows now because we out here fucking shit up. Bitch what's up with you?" I wanted to hang up and say nothing, but the tears came and I started crying as I tried to explain.

"He left me. Glitch left me and I don't know if he's coming back. You know I'm a stupid crazy bitch, I didn't mean it. Can you call him and tell him not to leave?"

"Bitch you beat that man with pots and pans, what you thought was gone happen. I actually thought he was gone beat your ass and leave you for dead. Wait, he didn't beat your ass did he?" Laughing through my tears, I knew she was the right person to call. I knew she would make me feel better.

"Best friend I just told you my man left me and your ass on my line cracking jokes. You know me so well. Thank you for not making this shit more depressing. Can you come over and drink with me, I need a male bashing night. We can talk about niggas and how they ain't shit."

"Oh, I'm on the way as soon as I drop granddaddy V off. I am with you on the bashing shit. This nigga got mad at me because I hit him and he bent me over and fucked me in the ass with donkey dick. I been limping all damn day. My ass feels like it got stretched out by a damn truck."

"What the fuck did you just say?" Hearing Uncle V bust in on her conversation had me in tears I was laughing so hard. Now that shit was worth the call.

"Daddy, get out of my conversation and finish dropping your tongues off. I'll be there in a lil bit. Make sure you got me a good pillow." Man I loved my best friend.

Getting up, I headed to the kitchen to put some wine in the fridge. Thinking it over, I grabbed some Hennessy and put that shit in the fridge as well. If we gone do the shit, I want to go all out. When I went to sit down, I thought about something. How the fuck was he leaving to get some space but didn't take his clothes? That means he been had to have some shit at that hoe house. It didn't matter what the fuck I did, his ass was leaving anyway.

What I did tonight just helped push him out of the door. This nigga thought he was slick, but I was about to go Bernadine on his ass. Running up the stairs, I grabbed his clothes and threw them on the lawn. It took me four trips to get his shit. Grabbing some lighter fluid out of the cabinet, I grabbed my Bic and headed outside.

I couldn't complete the look without this last item. Jumping in my car, I ran to the gas station and grabbed a pack of Newports. As soon as I got to my house, I stood over his shit. I was about to punk out and in my head, all I heard was get your shit. Get your shit and get out of my house. Hearing Bernadine voice in my head, I lit that shit with my Bic. Walking off, I lit up a cigarette and looked like a bad ass doing it. Glitch wanted to play, well fuck him.

Chapter Thirteen

REBECCA

*P*acing the floor, I had to try and calm my nerves. Vicious got me fucked up if he thinks I'm dumb enough to tell my men where I lay my head. His ass out there on a rampage taking my men out and cutting out tongues. I knew how he thought and that's why I set up the fake pick up.

They think because I'm a woman, I don't have the sense they do. See, I watched Vega for a long time which means I saw his mistakes as well. When he would fuck up, I would analyze over it for days until I figured out what he could have done to avoid it. Physically, they were a beast. Mentally, I was a savage and Vicious could never win against me.

Now that he thought he won, I was trying to figure out my next move. Right when the enemy thinks they are on top, you snatch they ass down and yell boom bitch. Knowing he was out there with Roulette, I got the perfect idea. Calling my driver, I got in and instructed them to take me to the ghetto bitch. It wasn't the cream of the crop, but it would definitely send the message I was trying to send. Pulling up to their house, we were about to get out when Roulette's right hand walked out. This was even better than the ghetto bitch. Roulette would cry over her friend, but this hood rat was the key to their entire organization. He practically ran the entire thing.

Whatever happened, he was so pissed, his ass never paid attention to us behind him. Ghetto ghetto must have shown her true colors, because only a woman can piss you off this much. We followed him all the way to the city. His ass pulled up at some broke down ass house and I knew it was now or never.

"Fernando, grab him quickly and quietly." Jumping out of the car, he did exactly what I asked. Watching him go down, a smile spread quickly across my face. This was going to be fun. After he threw him in the trunk, we headed back to the house. Getting out of the car, I walked with a new purpose.

"Set up the workshop please." Fernando smiled and went to get his tools. He loved doing twisted sick shit to people in order to get them to talk. I'm sure Glitch wouldn't, but I would have fun watching this show. Who knows, maybe after so much pain, he would have no choice but to give in. Heading down to the basement, I sat down in a chair not too far away from him. It took him about thirty minutes to wake up.

"Glad to see you finally woke up to join us. I thought you were a weak nigga and was gone go down from a punch to the head. You look confused. Do you know who I am?"

"From how you talk as if you are in charge, I would assume you're the bitch we're looking for." Laughing, I knew for a fact I was going to enjoy this.

"Good, then I don't have to tell you what kind of person I am. If you know what is best for you, then you will tell me what I need to know. Where is my son?" The confused look on his face let me know he had no idea what I was talking about. That just deemed him useless to me.

"Dead as far as I know."

"I believe you. I'm sorry, if you have no valid information for me, then you are of no value to me. You won't die for a long time and you will suffer greatly. Until I find my son, you will take the punishment every day until I do."

"You don't scare me. Do what the fuck you have to do. I'm built for this shit. When you live by the street, you die by them mother fuckers."

"I do have one more question for you. Why were you leaving the house so upset? It's not relevant to the conversation, I'm just curious. What did ghetto bitch do?"

"She didn't do anything. Now do what the fuck you have to do lil bitch." Nodding towards Fernando, he grabbed a hammer and hit him in the knee with it. Glitch screamed so loud, I thought he would pass out and die from one hit. It's funny how he said he was built for this. I hoped so, he had a long ride ahead of him. Standing up to leave, Fernando stopped me.

"Boss lady, what would you like me to do with him?" Rolling my eyes, I swear everyone around me was a bunch of dumb ass imbeciles. If I just said he was going to be tortured until I found my son, then that's what the fuck you do, torture him.

"I don't care what you do. Just remember, he is to stay alive until I find my son. Make sure he can't bleed to death or die from shock. If he dies, I promise you will regret it. Torture him and make it good." Rolling up his sleeves, he laughed and started grabbing some tools. Walking out, it felt good to win. While Vicious was out there getting useless information, he didn't realize he was losing the war.

Chapter Fourteen

CAPONE

I knew I wasn't going to see Roulette after that night. I didn't mean to fuck her up like that, but I needed her to know that I wasn't going to tolerate the bullshit. Now that I got my point across, I was regretting it. She hadn't even called to check on my progress. Since I was doing so good, I dismissed all the staff and it's just been me here.

Every day I have been waiting for her to walk through the door. Not only have she stayed the fuck away, but her deadline was approaching. I didn't want her to think I didn't have faith in her plan, but in two days, I was leaving this fucking house. It was time for me to start making moves and I needed to finally come back from the dead. Grabbing my phone, I dialed Shitz number.

"Either somebody playing a cruel ass joke, or somebody got the wrong damn number. Who the fuck is this?" I should have fucked with his ass, but it was more important things at stake here.

"It's me nigga. Look, I'm gone text you an address I need you to meet me at. Don't tell nobody you're coming and I mean nobody."

"How the fuck are you on the phone and I picked up your ashes? This some freaky shit."

"I'll explain it all when you get here. Just make sure you do what the fuck I said and come right now mother fucker."

"Say less." Shooting him a quick text, I gave him the address and headed to the shower. I wanted to be out and dressed before he got here. As soon as I was done with my hygiene, I got out and threw on some jeans and a T shirt. Throwing on my McQueens, I walked downstairs waiting for him to arrive. As soon the bell rung, I grabbed my gun and went to the door.

"Damn, you gone shoot me? I don't know whether to hug you or get the fuck up out of here. What up Cap." Giving him a quick hug, I let go because I wasn't with that homo shit. Heading to the den, we sat down. It was weird because his ass kept staring at me. Shit was making me feel uncomfortable. If his ass turned gay while I was gone, he was gone have to move the fuck around. I'm not a homophobe, but I wasn't about to be watching my booty every time my homie was around.

"Stop staring at me like that, shit don't feel right. You booty snatching?"

"Tell me what the fuck is going on before I shoot your ass myself."

"Just making sure. Now, my wounds wasn't life threatening. When I told you to get Roulette up there, she came. When she got up there, shorty say my mama was trying to kill me. Then went on to explain why she lit me the fuck up."

"That bitch lying. Why would your mama be trying to take you out, that don't make sense?"

"Same shit I said, until she told me why she lit me up. Vicious is the one that killed pops. My mama lied to everybody and that doesn't make sense at all. Why wouldn't you want revenge on the nigga that took your husband out? Once she found out Roulette was his daughter, she started pushing me to stay with her. She would say lil shit like you only here because I put you here. I'll handle Vicious you out of your league shit like that. I don't know the motive, but my mama moving flaw as fuck. Shorty didn't trust her coming back to the hospital again and moved me here. She faked my death to protect me from my mama and her daddy."

"Damn, that's some deep shit. Well, I guess shorty ain't as bad as I thought. She kept my nigga alive and I owe her one. Now, that the nice shit is out of the way, when you want to take your mama out?" I looked at this nigga like he was crazy. That's why we call him Shitz. He's always down to do whatever no matter who it is.

"You sound like shorty. Nobody is killing my mom but me. I need answers. What I can't figure out is how I tie into the story. Other than being her fucking son, what do I have to do with the revenge shit? Once I piece this shit together, if she flaw then you can take her out." Shaking his head, he relented.

"If she tried to kill you, we already know she flaw but whatever. What you need me to do, what's the plan?" That's where I got stuck. I didn't know what my next move should be. If I played my hand too fast with my mama, she could get the upper hand.

"That's why you here nigga. We need to figure out the right move before she finds out I'm still alive. I have to be ahead of her before she take my ass out. Right now we need to take advantage of the fact that she doesn't know I'm alive."

"You got me. I ain't never been shot let alone a ghost. You always been the thinker, I just enforce the shit. Get to thinking shit." He was right, but I thought for once his ass would have an idea other than going to the damn strip club. After thinking it over, I said fuck it.

"Take me to my mama. Best way to figure out what you want to know is to go to the source. Bitch don't scare me and I need to know what the fuck is going on."

"See, I knew you would figure it out. You ugly as fuck but you smart. Let's go. If at any moment you want to take that bitch out, just give me a head nod and her ass is done.:

"If my mama is going to die, it will be by my gun. I don't want that guilt on nobody else. Let's go."

"Say less." Heading out, we jumped in his car and I gave him directions to the hide out. The only reason I knew where it was because I pay the bills. Every month I get a bill for this property but my mama never spoke anything about it. Money wasn't a problem, so it never became an issue. Now I'm thinking she didn't want me to know for this very reason. The more I thought about it, the more I wanted to kill my fucking mama.

"We're a block away. Turn your headlights off and drive as slow as you can." He did what I asked and we parked. You could see movement in the house, but I don't know how many people were in there. Pulling our guns, we walked slowly up the stairs. Twisting the knob, it was open so we walked in. Fernando and my mama were sitting in the front talking about something. Conversation stopped when we walked in. She had the nerve to look happy.

"Oh my God, son you're alive. How? This is a miracle I can't believe it." She actually walked up on me and tried to give me a hug. Dodging that shit like gonorrhea, I side stepped her ass.

"Yeah, I'm alive no thanks to you. Tell me mother, how do I fit into your plan of revenge? I understand everything else, but why did you try to kill me? If Vicious killed dad, I get why you are upset. What I don't get is why you pushed me to date his daughter then tried to kill me like I was the fucking enemy." This crazy bitch actually started laughing.

"You're so fucking naïve. I should have known that little bitch saw me. Since the cat is out of the bag, I may as well tell you. At this point, I really don't give a fuck. You might want to sit down, you know you're weak. Don't want your knees to give out." My trigger finger itched like it never has before.

"Now Cap?" I almost laughed at Shitz. He was ready to take her ass out before I got the answer I needed.

"Naw, we gone sit our weak asses down and listen. Go head ma, tell me why you tried to kill your son."

"Twenty two years ago, I was your father's mistress. I did whatever the fuck he wanted me to do. When he wanted me to sleep with other men, I did it. I took the beatings, the embarrassment, and the miscarriages. The last time I was pregnant, he kicked the baby out of me. Said I wasn't built to be a parent. Vicious had a meeting with him and the plan was for me to fuck with him and find out everything and tell it to Vega. He was going to kill him and take over his operation.

Instead, Vicious came back and killed him. You were in the

room with him. You watched Vicious kill your dad. I always wondered if you would remember how your mother came in the room screaming. The sounds were killing my ears and I needed her to shut the fuck up. I had a plan and she was about to ruin it. Grabbing Vega's gun, I shot your mother right in the mouth and then in the head.

Out of nowhere, your father started coughing begging me to take him to the hospital. His bitch ass had survived the shooting and should have known he wouldn't go that easy. They always said you couldn't kill the devil but I did.

I raised my gun and shot that mother fucker until his face was no longer recognizable. Taking some shit out of the house, I made it look like a robbery. His team didn't know what to do and I took charge. I knew everything and they trusted me because I was always there. I've taken care of your bastard ass all these years and you weren't shit but an ungrateful, worthless, weak ass bitch. The one thing I needed you to do was get Vicious' daughter to fall for you. We were going to do what Vega tried to do, but I was going to succeed.

You couldn't do that and you let her damn near take you out. There was no use for you anymore. As soon as this is over, I'm going to finish what I started. Was that enough for you son." Looking over at Shitz, his face wore the same expression as mine. This bitch not only confessed to trying to kill me, but killing my parents as well. All these years I've always felt a disconnect to this bitch and now I knew why.

"You're telling me, that you aren't my mama?"

"Ain't that what the fuck I said. Do you know how hard it was pretending to love you? Vega killed every baby I got pregnant with, but I had to raise you. The woman I hated for so many years, I had to raise her fucking son."

"No you didn't. Why didn't you give me away?"

"Because his crew wouldn't have let me in if I did that. You were just a pawn at power. Now that I have it, I no longer need you." Not needing to hear anything else, I raised my gun at her. When Shitz saw me do that, he raised his as well.

"Do you think I'm about to let you walk the fuck up out of here? You have spent your last day on this mother fucker."

"Oh, I beg to differ. If you kill me, you will never be able to do the trade. Life for a life." Looking at Shitz, I think this bitch was trying to tell me she had Roulette. Grabbing my phone, I called her but she didn't pick up. Shit was going straight to voicemail.

"Where is she?"

"Calm down son. Everything will come to the light in due time. Just know, if you kill me the hood rat will starve to death and die from torture wounds." My heart dropped and I wanted to shoot this bitch face off her shoulders, but if I wanted to save Roulette, I had to let her leave.

"Stop calling me your son. If you touch her, I will make you suffer in a way that you have never seen."

"You're right. I'll be in touch bastard baby." We kept our guns pointed at her until she walked out of the door. Just the thought of them torturing her broke me down. Shitz pulled me off my feet forcing me to look at him.

"Ain't no time for tears bro. Pull it together so we can find your girl. When this is over, we will light that bitch up like bombs over Baghdad." Knowing he was right, I got my shit together and walked out. She would get hers. First I had to save my shorty.

Chapter Fifteen

ROULETTE

*K*nowing I was out of time with Capone, I had no idea what I was going to do. He was not going to stay hidden away and there was no way I could tell Vicious what I had done. The shit literally had me sick to my stomach. Throwing up in the toilet, this was the first time I ever felt fear. My crew would look at me as a traitor and there was no way they would allow me to be in charge after this. Even though it was my shit, they wouldn't allow someone like me to lead them anymore.

How could I have been so stupid? I should have told them what was going on. They didn't know where I had him hid so it wasn't like they could do anything. Vicious has been angry before, but this would be the first time he would be disappointed in me. As tears fell down my eyes, I threw up again.

"Okay bitch, I've heard enough. That shit ain't normal. You have been throwing up all morning and I'm taking your ass to the damn doctor. Get your ass up and stop feeling sorry for yourself. After we leave, we will go tell the crew together. I got your back and I won't allow anyone to do shit. Uncle V may kick you in the pussy, but you will live." Too sick to argue it, I got up and let her drive me to the doctor.

I was hoping we got there fast because everything about the car ride was making me feel fucked up. Right as I was about to throw up, the car stopped and I jumped out. Breezy would have killed me if I threw up in her shit. By the time we got inside, I could barely walk. Breezy held me up and I was grateful to have a friend like her. The emergency room was empty so it didn't take long for them to call me in the back.

After explaining everything that has been going on, they drew my blood and did a series of test. I've never been this sick in my life. My nerves were shot and I was scared of what it could be. This shit didn't feel like the flu.

"Bitch what if Capone gave me something? I'm gone kill his bitch ass. How the fuck you got donkey dick with a disease? What am I going to do?"

"Girl, he ain't gave you shit. Your ass got the flu or something. You gone be okay, I got you bitch. Even if your coochie is burning and itchy." We both laughed and it was a well needed distraction. Thirty minutes later, they were coming back in the room. Breezy squeezed my hand and we listened.

"Well Mrs. Barnes, we have figured out what was wrong with you. It seems that you have a little baby baking in the oven. Congrats mommy. You're about three months along. I'll set you up with a primary if you don't already have one so we can get you started on prenatal pills. Do you have any questions?" My ass was in shock and I didn't know what to say.

"No questions doc, thank you." The doctor walked out and my ass was frozen. "I'm about to be a God mommy. I'm so excited." I didn't know how to explain what I was feeling. I was about to be a mommy and I was excited about that, but how could I be Roulette and a mommy? Would Capone be happy about it? Would he be a deadbeat donkey or would he be excited.

"Breezy, what the fuck? This is a lot to take in with all that's going on. How the fuck am I going to be a mommy and I love toting guns and shit? Then on the other hand, I can't wait to hold the baby and smell it. Am I losing my mind?"

"Nope, but you about to lose your pussy bone. You have to

reveal two things to Uncle V today. Sucks to be you. Now let's go, we have to get this over with so we can find a reasonable solution."

"Have you heard from Glitch?"

"Nope, fuck him. I just pray I never run into him and that bitch. Don't worry about me right now, let's go." Walking out of the hospital, we got in the car and left. The drive to the warehouse was quiet. For some reason, it seemed like Breezy was speeding like a mother fucker. I wanted her to drive nice and slow, but her wheels was on crackhead time. When the car stopped, it took me forever to get out. "Bitch bring your scary ass on." Walking as fast as I could, we went in the warehouse. Vicious was beating one of the lil guys from my crew damn near to death. I had no idea what was going on in my shit anymore. I was losing my grip and I didn't like that feeling.

"Daddy, what are you doing?" When he saw me, his ass ran towards me and hugged me. Now my ass was confused and what I had to tell him was going to be harder than I thought.

"Your team is incompetent as fuck and I'm sick of it. The only reason I didn't kill his ass is because I didn't want to argue with you. Where the fuck have you been?" Looking at Breezy, it was now or never.

"Daddy, I have something to tell you." Before I could say it, Capone walked in the warehouse.

"Vicious we need to talk about Rou…" That's when he saw me. I was officially fucked. Everyone raised their guns on Capone and I knew I had to do something. Running in front of him, I threw my hands up to stop them.

"Daddy, it's my fault. That's what I was about to tell you. I didn't kill him and he didn't die. I hid him away because his mama tried to kill him and I needed to find out why." I hoped that would do the trick, but I was wrong as fuck. My daddy grabbed me by my neck and lifted my ass in the air. He was about to fuck me up, but Breezy started screaming.

"Please don't, she's pregnant." I could have killed the bitch myself. I know she thought she was helping me, but she just made it seemed like I saved his life because I was pregnant.

64

"Daddy I just found out thirty minutes ago." Putting me down, I've never seen him look so disappointed in my life. My daddy hated me right now and I don't blame him. I was looking flaw.

"Look, I know everybody is upset and confused right now, but I can clear everything up. I got the answers you were looking for." He went on to tell us the story that she told him. Everyone was speechless as fuck. "She told me she had you held hostage and that was the only reason I didn't kill her. Now that I know she doesn't have her, we can proceed to finding the bitch and kill her. What's the plan?"

"Now that we know you're not the enemy, we can go over a plan tomorrow. I guess you and my lying ass daughter can get some privacy. When you're done here, come to the fucking house and I will deal with you later." Pissed that he embarrassed me in front of everyone, I decided to piss him off more. Grabbing my gun, I aimed it at the floor.

"I'm sick of you talking to me like I'm a kid. I don't owe you an explanation and I'm not coming home. Oh, and take this with you." Pretending I was going to shoot him, I wanted to shoot the ground next to him. Capone decided to grab my arm when I pulled the trigger trying to stop me and made me shoot Vicious in the foot. This nigga was trying to get me killed.

"Mother fucker. You shot me in my fucking foot." Not wanting to look like a pussy, I acted as if I did it on purpose.

"Yea I shot you. Now what. I bet you shut your ass up next time."

"Shut your dumb ass up. You did the shit by accident. Get your simple ass over here and carry me all the way to the fucking hospital. If you let me fall, I will kick you in the pussy with my good foot." Running over to him, I'm glad he knew I didn't mean it.

"I'm so sorry daddy. I was trying to shoot the ground to scare you. I didn't mean to do it. I know you're mad at me, but I wasn't trying to keep nothing from you. I just wanted to try and make you proud by doing it on my own." I tried to use the proud card.

"If your lying ass don't get me to the hospital I promise you gone need a gurney too. Your ass wasn't trying to make me proud and how the fuck you was gone scare me shooting off a toe? Let's go." Laughing, I looked at Capone motioning for him to come with me. We had a lot to discuss.

Chapter Sixteen

VICIOUS

There wasn't a word to describe how pissed I was. Kalina had been lying, and then this bitch Rebecca was doing the most. All this time, I thought I had killed Vega. This bitch not only wiped him out, but she wanted to take out the entire operation. Her ass was in charge, but that wasn't enough. She wanted the streets as well.

A bitch like her wasn't the street type. How the hell do you run what you don't know about? See, I knew bitches like her. They were a dime a dozen. Fuck a nigga from the hood and they think they get street cred. Just because you lay with a boss, that doesn't make you a boss. I was tired of people having that mindset and think they ready to challenge the big dog.

I had mixed feelings about Kalina being pregnant. I've always wanted to be a grandfather, but I was just getting used to being out there in the trenches with her. I was looking forward to us being a force together and now I had to relinquish that idea. There was no way I was allowing her to be out there in those streets and she had a baby. It was time for her to let all this shit go. I did it for her, and she was going to do the same. All I had to do was figure out a way to convince her of that.

On top of all that bullshit, she done shot me in my damn foot. I don't know what it is about that foot, but the shit hurt like a mother fucker. I was being strong, but I had tears in my eyes. A nigga was praying for Jesus to take the wheel. He left that bitch right there, but it didn't stop me from asking. Now all of our dumb asses are sitting in the emergency room looking stupid. Kalina was constantly staring at me as if she was trying to read me and how I was feeling. Capone was staring at her as if he was trying to understand how it happened. Shit was a mess. They called my name and all of us stood up. Well I tried, but it hurt like hell.

"Look, I know yall here for me and you can come to the back after you're done talking. Right now, yall got some shit to discuss and my foot ain't that important."

"You sure? I don't want you to be by yourself. Me and Capone can talk later. I want to make sure my daddy good. Anything else really can wait." Kalina was trying to use me as an excuse to get out of talking to Capone.

"I'm sure. Besides, you're the one that did it. You think you slick. Your ass done got pregnant and think I can't kick you in the pussy. I'll hold this wheel chair and use my other foot. So, it might be safer for you out here." Thinking it over, she agreed and allowed me in the back. As soon as I was out of ear shot, my ass started begging.

"Excuse me nurse, do you think I can get some pain meds? I'm dying over here." The nurse laughed and nodded her head.

"You look like a strong man, I'm sure you can take it. Besides, it's just your foot. It's not going to kill you, man up." I almost slapped her ass across the room for that comment. Now my ass had to pretend I was good so she don't think I was some punk ass nigga.

"If I bent your ass over, I bet you won't be talking shit." When she laughed, that gave me the green light to keep fucking with her. It took my mind off the pain.

"What's your name? I like to know who a person is before I kill them out."

"Melissa, yours?" Wondering if I should tell her my real name or my street name, I decided on the latter. Either you were going to accept me for who I was, or we could move around and forget we ever met each other. One thing I knew for sure was, there was no more hiding.

"Vicious." You could tell she had heard about me and in a strange way, that made me feel good about myself.

"Thee Vicious. Like the serial killer?" I couldn't do shit but laugh at that. I was about to say I wasn't no damn serial killer, but I guess you can say I was. I have a signature and I stay bodying niggas.

"Yeah that's me. How the fuck someone like you know about someone like me?" Now it was her turn to laugh.

"Just because I did something with my life, doesn't mean I didn't come from the hood. I was born and raised in K Town. Your ass may be tough, but you don't want to fuck with me." You could tell she was lying. She didn't know shit about the hood.

"Okay tough girl, can I take you out when my foot heals?"

"It all depends on what you're working with when I help you change into your gown." I damn near choked at how bold she was. I'm glad a nigga wasn't short in that department. Not even waiting on her help, I stripped out of my clothes and put my gown on. When I laid back in the bed, I made sure my gown stopped above my dick. Her eyes got big and I could tell she was nervous.

"You can put that thing up now."

"Naw, you do it." Looking around, she grabbed my dick and released it fast as hell. Pulling my gown down, she was nervous as hell.

"I'll give you my number when you get back from x-rays. Someone should be coming to get you shortly." As she walked out of the room, I admired her ass. It wasn't too big and not too small. Shit was just right and I couldn't wait to get up in those guts. Now that I had nobody to talk to, it seem like my pain came back. That shit hit me so hard, I could feel it in my dick. Since I didn't want her to think I was a bitch, my ass suffered for it. As she said, someone came in and took me to x-rays and by the time I came back to my room, I was in so much pain, I didn't give a fuck who knew it. A nigga was pushing the shit out of that button.

"Somebody better come in here and bring me some pain meds

before I blow this shit up. My damn foot hurt shit. Where the fuck is the damn doctor? Can yall hear me in here? Fuck are yall doing?"

"The entire hospital hears your sissy ass. I know Vicious not in here crying over a lil shot to his foot. I should have recorded this for the next time he tries to take over my camp." Kalina and Capone walked in catching me in a weak moment.

"Fuck you. I didn't say shit when you was trying to slip and slide because your ass was hurting. What happened to your ass again? Her and Capone damn near choked and I knew exactly what happened. "Yall some nasty ass bitches. Get the fuck out of my room." They laughed as if I was playing, but I should have shut the fuck up. Nobody wanted to know that shit. My crew walked in and even though I was happy, I didn't want them to see me weak. Until I noticed that E Way had a limp, everybody knew Grew had a shaky hand, so I didn't feel so bad.

"Bae we gone start calling they ass the handicap hitters. They old ass don't stand a chance out there in these streets." We all laughed and it was good having my family together. Grew walked up to Capone and reached out his hand.

"What's up, I'm Kalina's uncle Grew. How you doing youngblood?"

"NOOOO." Everyone yelled out at the same time and Grew got mad as hell.

"I will bet you ten racks that nigga got piss on his hand. Don't do it Capone." Looking from me to Kalina, he realized we were serious and dropped his hand.

"Fuck yall." We all bust out laughing again and I noticed the pain was gone again. My family was taking my mind off of the shit and I was grateful to them. A nigga needed it to, because that pain was about to take me out. Melissa walked in and I immediately started smiling.

"You missed me already huh?"

"Naw, the entire floor heard you crying and begged me to come give you some meds." If I didn't want her so bad, I would have been like fuck her. She embarrassed the shit out of me.

"Say it ain't so V." E Way was laughing a lil too hard for me.

"I bet I could still fuck your mama."

"I bet you can too. She Senile with no teeth and got chin hair. She been waiting on a sucker like you to prove a point." We all shared another laugh, but this time Melissa joined in. For some reason, the shit just felt right.

Chapter Seventeen

BREEZY

*E*verybody was happy and finding their true love, but my ass was trying to figure out where the fuck my nigga was. I still can't believe this is what my life had become. It's been a couple of weeks and I hadn't heard from Glitch. Nigga didn't even attempt to come back for the rest of his clothes.

I even found out I was pregnant, but I kept the shit to myself. In another day, this would have been ideal. Me and my best friend having a baby at the same time, that shit would have been lit as fuck. Now, my ass was sitting here crying trying to figure out how got I here. We had our future planned and now I didn't know if I still wanted to be here. It had to be a better life than this. I was starting to think if I wanted a better life, I needed to leave this place.

I know that my best friend would be disappointed and upset, but this was a decision I needed to make for me. My father was gone, Glitch disappeared and I don't want to look like the depressed friend jealous of everyone else that is doing great. I was extremely happy for everyone, and I needed them to know that. Sitting around being depressed would only make them feel I wasn't. We were about to have a meeting and I knew they were going to be upset, but on today, I would be telling everyone that I was out of here.

Grabbing my purse, I jumped in my car and headed towards the warehouse. The tears filled my eyes and it's as if I was engulfed in pain. The world was closing in on me and I couldn't catch my breath. Pulling over on the side of the road, I broke down. Nothing good ever happened to me and I just didn't understand. All my life I lived my life how I wanted to. The rebellion towards my father gave me the edge to live life freely.

Now, karma was beating my ass for all the shit I've done. That had to be the answer to my problems. The shit I did was coming back to bite me in the ass. Finally getting my breathing under control, I pulled off and headed towards the warehouse again. It was time to get this shit over with, so I could go on about my way. My ass had enough money to live three lifetimes. I could go anywhere in the world, why would I stay here and be depressed. Pulling up, I felt myself going into a panic but I refused to keep being a coward.

Getting in the car, I walked in and everyone was gearing up for war. I wanted to scream no this isn't safe for our babies, but Roulette was leading the pack. How could she willingly put her baby in harm's way without a second thought. This was what I needed to get away from.

"Breezy I'm glad that you are here. Grab that bag of guns off the table. Most people hide in plain sight, since Capone already saw her in the hideaway, we would assume she wouldn't go back. That may be exactly where she is, so we are heading over there. Grab those guns off the table and the bag of ammo. We don't know what we are walking into, so we will be war ready. My daddy is not one hundred but insists on going. We will need to cover his weight."

"You don't need to cover shit. I keep telling you I'm good. Say that shit again and I will make your ass stay here. Breezy quit looking slow and grab the shit. We have to go, now."

"When this is over, I'm leaving. Not the warehouse, but Chicago for good. No need for any follow up questions or responses, let's get this shit over and done with." Everyone had shocked looks on their face, but I grabbed the bag and stormed out of the warehouse. It could have been the hormones, but I was over this shit.

Everyone piled into their cars and followed each other to the house. They knew damn well this bitch wasn't here, but we were going on a wild goose chase anyway. This shit was irritating the fuck out of me, but the longer it took to go in this empty as house, the longer it was going to take for me to leave. Seeing everyone else get out of their cars, I got out of mine and followed suit into the house.

Everyone went searching, but it was clear the house was empty. Stopping in the kitchen, I grabbed some chips off the table and started eating them. When I realize the house got quiet, I assumed they left forgetting I was even there. Sitting down at the table, I decided to finish my chips.

"BREEZY COME DOWNSTAIRS. FRIEND HURRY UP OH MY GOD." Eating another chip, I slowly made my way downstairs. Guess they bitch ass didn't leave after all. When I made it to the bottom of the stairs, I threw up everything I had just eaten.

"Is that.. There is no way that is. Oh God. Oh my God. Please tell me that's not him." Glitch was covered in blood. He had holes everywhere and his hands were smashed in. You could barely recognize him. Running over to him, I worked hard at untying him. All this time I thought he had left me, but he was here. He had to be. I know there is no way he would leave me. As soon as all of the restraints were off, his body dropped out of the chair. Not because he didn't have balance, but as if he was dead. His body just dropped. Me and Roulette screamed.

"Capone get the women out of here and let's clean this up. They are not strong enough to be here." Normally, we would have cursed him out but he was right. There was no way I could see Glitch in that way and I'm sure Roulette felt the same. We barely made it up the stairs and I felt as if I was going to pass out. I couldn't believe this was happening to me again. How could Glitch be dead? Why would she kill him? My baby was going to be without a father and I had no idea what to tell her. Yes, I was claiming a her.

"Breezy I am so sorry. If we hadn't come back, we wouldn't have known that he was here all this time. I'm sorry that you had to see that, I'm sorry that he is gone. I don't know how we can get past this. Oh my God this is too much. Fuck." Grabbing me, we held each other and cried. My father was the biggest lost I ever had to deal with, but Glitch dying and me still not over my father was too much. Hearing the guys come up the stairs, we buried our faces in each other's chest so we didn't have to see his body. I couldn't see him like that again.

"Get your cry baby asses up and help us. Baby girl get my keys out of my pocket and open the truck doors. You're gonna have to drive, but Roulette, I need you to drive like you have never driven before." We both looked confused as to what Uncle V was saying. Noticing that we didn't understand, he started yelling again. "He is alive. The pulse is barely there, but Capone felt it. If we want to save him, we have to move now."

"If fast is what we need, then I'm driving the Bugatti. Capone, drive my daddy's truck so we don't leave it here. Breezy, ride with me. Just in case you get left behind, I'm going to Rush. Let's go." Everyone ran out and followed the orders that Roulette barked out. It was no time for a power struggle and we wanted to save Glitch.

Once we were on the road, I held onto Glitch as tight as I could. I needed him to know that I was there. I needed him to know that he had his family. He fought all this time to hold on for something, so he could fight some more. I was giving him a reason to fight.

"I'm here baby. Don't worry, I'm here. I love you and I'm sorry for everything, please don't leave me. We have so much to fight for. Please baby, don't leave me." I heard tires burning and looked out of the window. I think this bitch got us here in five minutes. She wasn't playing no games.

"Baby girl if I find out that's how you been driving my fucking car, I'm gone beat your ass. Get a nurse and a damn gurney." She didn't respond, and I was glad she didn't. Her and Uncle V could argue for hours. Glitch needed to be inside and then they can go at each other over a car they can buy a million times. It seemed like the entire hospital staff came running out and it looked intimidating. They grabbed Glitch and took him inside. This was going to be one hell of a fight and I prayed he didn't give up.

Sitting down in the waiting room, it seemed like everyone was lost in their own thoughts. Nobody knew what to say and the silence was like a ticking clock. It's like the doctor could came any minute and tell us he was dead. I'm not sure that I could survive this if he died. All the shit that we had done in our life, all the people that we have killed. The city feared us, but this bitch didn't. Out of all the people that feared us, the one time we needed them too, they didn't. I was so hurt and pissed, I had no idea what to do as I waited. Out of nowhere, I started singing Sweet Architect by Emeli Sandé. Not loud, but enough to heal my heart.

Oh, sweet architect my bones are heavy and my soul's a mess. Come find my address and build me up build me up. Oh, sweet architect I've been lonely since the day you left. So, come find my address. Build me up build me up.

In my mind, everyone was in the room singing with me and Glitch would be able to hear us. He would feel the love he had out here waiting. A group of people hurting and broken. We all were coming together trying to heal, but when I opened my eyes, everyone was looking at me like I was crazy.

"Girl if you don't shut the fuck up, they gone put us out of here. I know you are hurting because we can hear it, but damn girl. I'm about to let you join handicap hitters. Kalina, get the strap." Everyone including me started laughing. Uncle V said enough lil bitch and it was funny as hell. I needed that laugh. Roulette sat next to me and held my hand. Something so simple, can mean so much. Without her saying a word, that helped calm my nerves. Uncle V going off, helped me take my mind off the situation and we all were one big family. Leaning and depending on each other.

Six hours later, a doctor walked towards us looking perplexed. My heart stopped and I knew there was no way he was bringing me good news. The tears started to flow and I knew my life was about to change forever. The doctor continued to talk and each word broke me down. I think I let out a scream, but I wasn't sure. All I remember is falling to the ground feeling a pain I had never felt. *Build me up build me up.*

~

Sitting beside Glitch, I couldn't stop crying. Roulette had to fill me in on what the doctor said since I fell the fuck out. His hands were damn near mangled. It's a possibility that he may never regain function in them. Bullet wounds to the neck, chest, stomach, and both knees. He may never regain function in his legs. After they shot him in the knees, they beat him with hammers. They don't have any idea how long he has been like that, but they know it's been at least two weeks. His blood lost was massive and they had to give him a transfusion. They felt it was a miracle that he held on this long.

"Glitch, just know that I am here. I'm not leaving you I promise. No matter what the road is ahead. I will be here for you. Just know that I love you and if you can hear me I need for you to fight. I'm pregnant and I don't want to do this alone. The baby needs you, I need you. Roulette needs you. Please don't leave us.

Yeah we're still here and we're still breathing. Knee deep with a deep needing. We stay brave though we've been damaged. See most got a heart, but some savage. Oh, dear heaven I hope you're up to something. Cause dear heaven this just can't be for nothing. Build me up build me up.

"Best friend, what is this song you keep singing? I've never heard it, but it sounds amazing. Well, your voice doesn't but I love the lyrics to the song. You keep singing it and I want to know why? Does it have any meaning?"

"On Love and Hip Hop somebody died and they played the song while they were at the funeral. For me it means that it had to be some kind of purpose for God's plan. Whatever his will is, I have no choice but to accept it but my body and soul can't take it. I need our architect to come build me up. Whatever is going on, I am being torn down. Ripped apart. Dragged all over the fucking place. It has to be a reason behind this, God wants this for me. In order for me to take this pain that I keep enduring, I need him to build me up."

"Oh my God friend, I'm so sorry. I have been a bad friend. You lost your dad and we moved on with our lives. You thought Glitch left, and I threw my baby and happiness in your face. Not on purpose, but we are just living as if you're not hurting. I'm so sorry. He will build you up and what he doesn't do, I will pick up the slack. You don't have to leave, I will always be here for you. Glitch knows that. He will come back to us and if he doesn't, I will be right there with you to keep picking up the pieces until you are okay. If you want to walk around in mix match shoes, I'm okay with that friend. God got us. We just have to know that. We aren't bad people, we chose to live a way of life. I would like to believe that God still loves us all. You sound like shit but keep singing. He needs to hear your voice and know that you are here.

I needed that, I'm glad that she understood what I needed and wanted to hear. My heart was shattering and it seemed as if no one cared. Everyone moved on while I fell to pieces. I'm glad my friend said this. It helped me fight harder.

Build me up build me up.

Chapter Eighteen

CAPONE

*a*ll this shit was going on, and I haven't gotten the chance to even process the fact that I was having a baby. Even though me and Roulette talked about it, shit didn't go as planned. Vicious was taken in the back to get his foot looked at when Roulette shot him. As soon as he was carried away, I turned to her for answers.

"If I hadn't been at the warehouse when Breezy screamed that out, would you have told me or would you have kept me in the dark?" From the way that she stayed silent for a while, I assumed I was right. It took her about three minutes to speak up.

"It's complicated. My father wanted you dead, I wasn't sure how much I could trust you and my hormones were all over the place. I don't know if you even want to be a father. What did you expect me to do? Two days ago, I was ready to fight my father for my legacy. Today, I find out that I am a mother. I have no experience at this because I've never had a mother." Hearing her say that brought me back to who I was dealing with. I got what she was saying, but I also knew she was telling me that my ass wasn't going to find out.

"I know that you are scared, hell, everything that I thought I knew just went out the window. I have no idea who I am anymore, but this is one thing I do know. I will do everything in my power to give that baby everything. I will be the

best parent I can and keep fighting to be better. No one truly knows how to be a great parent. All this shit is trial and error."

"Fuck that. I'm Roulette. I'm supposed to be good at everything, but I'm scared about this. I have no idea what it is to be a mother. I've never seen anyone be a mother. I don't want to fail."

"Do you hear yourself Shorty? If you're sitting here saying that you don't want to fail, that means you care enough to fight. That's all that matters. All you have to do is be willing to fight." When I still saw the uncertainty in her eyes, I got pissed off. Snatching her to the bathroom, I forced her clothes down.

"Oh no Donkey dick, we not about to do this shit again. I can't take that and you shouldn't want to hurt the mother of your child." Laughing, I rubbed her pussy. Bringing my hand to my mouth, I licked it making sure it was wet. Slapping her pussy, she jumped in confusion.

"What the fuck are you doing? Your ass always on some punishment type shit. Can you just lick it and let me nut that way?" Ignoring her, I slapped her on the clit again. She winced but a moan followed after.

"Are you going to try and be a great mother or are you going to keep bitching and complaining?" No answer was given so I slapped her against her pussy a little harder.

"Yes, I am going to try."

"Fuck that. Tell me you are going to be a great mother to our child." She didn't respond so I grabbed her clit and pinched it a little.

"I'm going to be a great mother to our child." Seeing that she got my point, I picked her up and slid her down on my dick. I missed her pussy so much and I needed this shit like I needed air. I'm glad that she no longer fights me on us sleeping together. Tearing into her pussy, I damn near died three times in that shit. Feeling her cum all over me, I was able to release without feeling bad. Lowering her on the sink, I kissed her and prayed she felt my love for her.

That was the first night and we barely spoke about the baby sense. I want to be happy, but I don't know if she even plans on keeping the baby. The way that she goes running out in the streets without a second thought, tells me she doesn't want that. Seeing her kick in doors toting guns have me nervous as fuck. I wanted to scream a million times mother fucker sit your ass down, but I knew she would only fight against that.

With Roulette, you had to strategize. You couldn't say shit to her directly, we had to figure out ways to trick her into doing the shit that we wanted her to do. She thought I didn't know that she had a doctor's appointment, but I had been following her. Seeing her get out of the car made me feel some type of way. Knowing how far along she was, they were about to tell her the sex of the baby.

That alone had me so mad, I reacted without thinking. Running up to her, I grabbed her so fast, she pulled a gun on me. You could see the startled look on her face when she realized it was me. Then the ashamed look came. She knew that I was pissed, but I didn't have time to pacify her feelings.

"That is my child in there. Unless you want to make a fucking confession to me, that is my child. You do not get to keep me in the dark. You do not get to make decisions without me. YOU DO NOT GET TO FIND OUT THE SEX WITHOUT ME. I will fuck you up so bad, they will have to take the baby out of your throat. Are we clear?"

"I have heartburn. My appointment is not until next week, but since we are here I can ask them if we can do it today. My ass was burping, farting, and chest burning too much. I needed something and I came here. If you ever grab me again, I will…" She saw my petty face and knew to shut the fuck up. I wish she would have threatened me like I was some worker that fucked up. I was tired of this power struggle with her, but it was one of the things that brought us closer together.

"Let's go."

Waiting for the doctor to come in had me nervous as hell. I wasn't sure if Roulette really heard me or if she thought she could do what she wanted. I don't know shit about babies or how this works, but I'm going to give it my all. I'm not sure that Shorty would do the same. The doctor came in and my ass was ready to pass out.

After explaining that heart burn comes with the pregnancy, she laid her down and rubbed some jelly on her. I had no idea what was happening until the baby popped up on the screen. The thing was ugly and I prayed that's not how it was going to come out. I thought

I was a nice looking nigga and I know Shorty is. How the hell could our baby come out looking like this.

"Excuse me doc. Is that how our baby is going to look?" They both laughed before the doctor responded, so I knew my question was dumb. They ass better not say shit smart or Shorty was going to pay for it. They knew my ass didn't know this shit.

"No, your baby won't look like this. Okay, have you two decided yet?" Roulette shook her head yes, but they had me fucked up. I knew Shorty was gone try this shit, but it wasn't happening.

"If you think I'm gone sit here and let you kill my baby you got me fucked up. Doc, I know you don't know who the fuck I am, but you will if you attempt to kill my baby. I promise you and your family won't make it til tomorrow." The doctor damn near choked and Roulette looked outright embarrassed. Now I was confused.

"Umm, I was asking did you decide if you wanted to know the sex of the baby. It's too late for her to terminate at this point. It's not many doctors that would do that procedure. Your threat wasn't necessary. I'm not sure if I can be your Primary after a threat like that." I felt dumb, but I meant what I said.

"Are you the best doctor for my baby?" She nodded her head yes and I continued. "Then you will be her doctor if you don't want to upset me. This is my first time, it's some stuff I don't know. Just try to explain it to me. Now, continue and tell us the sex of our baby please." She cleared her throat and continued to move the thing on her stomach. Roulette stayed quiet.

"Well, it looks like you are going to have a boy." The wind hit me in my chest and I had no idea something that small could feel so good. I couldn't stop the tears, but I tried to hold them back. I didn't want Shorty to think I was weak. I've just never felt like this before. This was a different type of love. Hugging Shorty, I didn't want to ever let her go. The doctor gave us a print out and thanked us for our time. Once she was gone, I wiped Shorty off and watched her get dressed.

"I love you girl. Your ass stuck now and it ain't shit you can do about it." Laughing, she responded as well.

"I love you too. Walking out the office hand in hand, nothing could take my happiness away. At least I thought until I saw the bitch from my mama's kitchen standing by our cars. Pulling my gun, it was funny to see Shorty pulled hers as well. We were gone have to talk about this shit. Once this was over, I wanted her to let all of this shit go.

"What the fuck do you want? Is she here?" Shorty was looking at me confused.

"Wait. How do you know Lisa?" Now I was confused.

"She was at my mama's house. How do you know her?" Shorty went on to explain how she knew her. I knew it was something about that bitch when I saw her at my table. If I didn't know anything else, I know she can tell me where Rebecca is. I had to learn to quit calling that bitch my mama. Back to the situation at hand, I kept my gun on her and asked my question again.

"Why are you here?"

"I came to bring you a present. I'm going to tell you where to find your mother. What she is doing, what she has planned is wrong and I can't be a part of that. Her plan is to stay hidden until your baby is born and then kill it. I'm not a monster and I want no parts of that shit. If you leave me be, I'll tell you where to find her. We have to do this quickly because she follows you most of the time. I think she has tracking on your car.

"Tell me where she is and you are safe." Lisa handed me a paper that I looked over and motioned for her to leave.

"Do you trust her?" Shorty was looking skeptical and she was right, it could have been a set up. One thing I did know was, I needed to see where Lisa rested her head just in case she was.

"I don't know, but we will find out."

Chapter Nineteen

VICIOUS

*I*t was too much going on in our camp. This shit with Glitch had me pissed and here I was out in the city killing innocent people. Well, not really innocent but they had nothing to do with the situation. There were no velvet boxes, just pain and quick kills. I could have chosen to use my gun, but I needed to feel the death. I needed to feel the person take their last breath under my hands.

It was mean and cruel, but in this moment, it's what I needed. Seeing this nigga from back in the day that I know was an undercover, I jumped out and ran up on him. You could tell I startled him and I didn't give a fuck about none of the logistics and small talk.

"Vicious what the fuck. You scared the fuck out of me. I heard you back but I didn't believe it. It's good to see you man." By the time he got his last word out, I stuck my knife in as far as it could go. I swiped across as aggressive as I could. Feeling his Adam's apple and wind pipe crushing, I felt a rush. Allowing him to drop to the floor, I watched as blood poured from his neck. The shit felt good and I don't know how I ever gave this shit up. Blood was all over me and I didn't give a fuck. Jumping in my car, I was looking for my next victim. When my phone rung, I almost didn't answer it. I wanted to feel as if I wasn't just sitting around waiting to find Rebecca. Seeing it was Roulette, I answered.

"What's up baby girl, I'm kind of in the middle of something."

"Dad, get to the house right now. Not after you finish doing pointless shit and don't lie. I know you and I know what you are doing. It's not helping. I have what you are looking for. Get here now." Knowing the only thing I wanted was Rebecca, she had to have news on her whereabouts. My ass damn near had five accidents on the way home.

Running in the house, Kalina was sitting on the couch with Capone. Rebecca was nowhere in sight, so I was confused on what she meant by she had her. I wasn't about to play this game with them. If they were worried about me, they can keep that shit. I should have known better when they said meet here and not at the warehouse.

"Where is she?" Kalina looked to Capone, she wanted him to explain what was going on.

"Lisa approached us at the doctor saying Rebecca has a tracking on me. She follows me from time to time and knows that we are having a baby. When Shorty gives birth, she plans to kill him. Lisa said she wanted no parts of that shit and if she gave us Rebecca's whereabouts, would we allow her to live and I agreed. The problem is, we don't know if we can trust her. We followed her home and Rebecca was nowhere in sight. She's staying at a run down hotel like she is trying to hide out. It can be a set up and we walk into a massacre or she could be telling the truth. What do you think."

"I think I ain't never ran from a nigga and I'm damn sure ain't about to pick today to start running." They looked shocked like I shouldn't be quoting Lil Wayne. "There ain't a damn thing Rebecca can do that we aren't ready for. Let's end this and go on about our way. I'm tired of looking for her ass and I'm sure all the people I was about to kill will appreciate that shit. You are going to have a baby and we need to get this shit out of the way. Breezy is out. She needs to be there for Glitch. Get the rest of the crew together, we meet in an hour. We don't give her a chance to leave."

"Shorty, can you sit this one out as well?" I almost laughed at

Capone. I appreciate him trying, but I could have told his ass it was no way in hell she would agree to that.

"Nigga please. Don't start doing that shit. I'm good." You could tell he wanted to say more, but he just clenched his jaw and stayed quiet. I felt the same way he did, but this was not the time to argue with her, we had to get moving.

"Go, what the fuck are you waiting on. See you in a minute."

"Say less." Capone grabbed Kalina and they walked out. Going upstairs, I jumped in the shower to wash the blood off from my night of fun. I wanted to be fresh as fuck for this bitch Rebecca. She deserved to have her blood all by itself. Once I was done, I went in the closet and got dressed. Putting on all black, I felt like this was going to be the closure I needed. I refused to go and see Fat Back until I had avenged him. My phone rang and I answered. It was Melissa.

"What's up sexy." You could tell she was blushing through the phone.

"I wanted to know if you would like to join me for dinner. I want to get to know you, but you kind of disappeared on me."

"I'm sorry, but I'm gone have to get a rain check."

"Fuck. You were just flirting. You didn't really want to date me. I'm so sorry to have bothered you."

"Shut your sensitive ass up. I have some business to take care of, trust me, I got you. There is no way I'm letting all that ass get away from me." She was quiet for a minute and then she asked me a question I wasn't sure she wanted the answer to.

"Are you going to kill someone?"

"Do you really want to know that sexy?"

"Yes, I do. If we are going to date, I need to know who I'm dating." Thinking it over, I decided to give her what she wanted.

"I'm not going to kill someone. I'm going to torture and destroy someone. I've never wanted to kill someone so bad in my life."

"Keep going." When I heard the wet sounds, I kind of froze. If my ears were still working correctly, she was playing in her pussy as I talked about killing someone.

"I want to snatch her head off her body while she is in the

middle of begging for her life. I want to take every piece of her body apart and watch her bleed to death."

"Yes daddy. What else." This had to be the strangest shit I ever did.

"I want to watch the blood pour from her body as she gasps for air. This will be long and painful and I need to see the pain in her eyes.

"Oh fuck. I'm cumming daddy." My dick was brick hard and if it wasn't Rebecca, I would be at her door trying to fuck her brains out. She had no idea what she was doing to me. No woman ever made me want to cum this bad, not even Kelly.

"If I'm gone be able to do all of this, I need to get going. You about to fuck my head up. I'll call you when I'm done." Hanging up, I pulled my dick out and jacked off in the truck. I had to release my nut or my ass would go to this shit with my head all fucked up.

Chapter Twenty

I've been sitting in the hospital since Glitch was admitted. My ass was funky and I'm sure I looked a mess. I refused to leave and I appreciated Roulette and Uncle V coming to check on me bringing food and shit. I didn't want the baby to suffer because of my depression. I had to be strong for Glitch and the baby.

He was awake, but he hadn't said a word since. Not one movement or one single word. The doctors said this may be his life permanently. I couldn't fathom not ever hearing his voice again. The shit was fucking me up, but I refused to cry in front of him. Glitch needed me and I was determined to be strong for him. He needed to know he had someone.

"Hey best friend, hey Glitch. I wanted to stop by to see if you needed anything before we headed out. You good?"

"I'm okay for now, but later you can bring me some Popeyes. I've been craving that shit. Wait. Where are you going?" She hesitated and I knew she didn't want me to know. Turning towards her all the way, I wanted her to know she better not lie to me. Seeing the intense look on my face, I guess she decided to tell me the truth.

"We may have found out where Rebecca is. My daddy told me

you can't go and I wasn't supposed to tell you. He wanted you here with Glitch and I don't blame him. If it's a set up, we don't want him here by his self. Bitch you smell bad, what the fuck."

"Fuck you and tell Uncle V, he got me fucked up. Do you see the love of my life? Do you see what that bitch did to him? She killed my daddy and tried to kill my fiancé. There is no way I'm not in on this kill. All the kills you took me on that was pointless and had nothing to do with me, I went with no problems. Now, the one that matters to me the most, you try to shut me out. Why?"

"Best friend I promise it has nothing to do with anything other than what I said. We found out the location from Lisa. If she is lying and it's a set up, they could try to come after Glitch knowing we left him to go there. We didn't want them to do anything else to him. He's been through hell and we love him. Please understand that." Taking a deep breath, I knew what she was saying was the truth. If they came back and finished the job, I would never forgive myself.

"Okay, but I promise you better make that bitch suffer. She doesn't get to go easily. My fiancé went through torture for days, she does not get to get off with a bullet. Tell Uncle V he better hurt her bad."

"Best Friend you want me to cut her toes off and remove her eyes then leave her alive. You know how fucked up her life would be with no toes. Bitch would be clumsy as fuck and can't see where she going." We laughed, but we both knew she couldn't stay alive.

"That bitch better not leave out of there alive. Don't play with me. Now hurry up and update me as soon as you're done." Hugging me, she walked out and left me to deal with my thoughts.

"Where is Breezy." Glitch was talking, but I guess he didn't know that I was in the room. I couldn't believe he was talking even though he wasn't talking loudly.

"I'm here baby. I knew you would talk to me again. There was no way you would leave my talkative ass to talk by myself forever."

"Shut the fuck up. I know you're here. I'm asking where is the Breezy that I know. My Breezy wouldn't allow anyone to hurt me. I could have been said something to you, but I was embarrassed. How do you say to someone that you're embarrassed? That you feel weak because you let the bitch get the best of you. Two times in one day, a woman took me down. I needed to heal so that I could fuck her up in the worst way.

That's something I may never get to do. You have the chance to do that. Why wouldn't you? Don't let her get away with what she did to me. They don't get to make that decision. You make them make her suffer. You deserve to be there just as much as them. Go be Breezy."

"As much as I want to be there, I don't want to lose you. If she comes back, I will kill myself for not being here. Please don't make me choose." You could tell he was getting frustrated.

"Look at me. I may never walk or use my hands again. If that bitch came back, what more can she do to me. I may not hold my baby Breezy. I may never have sex with you again and that alone is killing me. I need you to make sure she suffers. Please." Knowing how badly he needed this, I made my decision.

"I'll go baby. I'll go. If you let that bitch come in here and kill you, I'll barge in heaven and beat your ass. Right in front of Jesus and I'm not playing." Bending down, I kissed him and walked out. I knew I had to drive fast if I wanted to catch them. There was no way I could come back and tell him I wasn't there.

Seeing all the cars still at the warehouse, I knew I made it in time. Getting out the car, I took a deep breath. I've never gone against Uncle V's wishes and I didn't feel like arguing with him. He was intimidating and he usually got what he wanted. Roulette knew how to get him to bend, but I'm not sure if we had the same relationship. I didn't want him to embarrass me in front of the workers. I just needed him to understand and let me do this. Walking inside, everyone stopped and looked at me.

"Boo, you don't need to be here. We got this, just make sure Glitch is straight."

"Uncle V, I know I don't have to be, but I need to be. Glitch wants me to be here. So, let's just do this. No questions and no debates. Pass me some guns and ammo and let's go. Oh, and glitch said she better suffer." Seeing Uncle V nod and hand me what I needed made me feel good.

"You not riding with though. Your ass smell like the free clinic. I'm nowhere near you and I can smell you from over here. Before you go back up there with Glitch, clean yourself up. I wouldn't walk either if that's what I had waiting to hug me." Everyone laughed, but me. I ran towards him and gave him a big ass hug. Now he smelled like me too.

"Now you smell like a homeless cripple. Let's go. If she catch you because your ass can't keep up, I'm gone leave your ass right there." We all laughed as we walked out of the warehouse. It was time to take this bitch down once and for all.

Getting in my own car, I prayed that this bitch wasn't going to the hospital to get Glitch. I needed him and my baby needed him. She had taken enough and she don't get to take anymore. All I wanted was one piece of happiness, and I needed this to be that moment. If it wasn't, I know I would completely break. When my daddy died, he died disappointed in me. I needed to do something that will make him proud of me. Avenging him and Glitch would mean that it wasn't for nothing. My daddy could smile down on me and I needed that closure.

Chapter Twenty-One

ROULETTE

I would never give my father the satisfaction of saying this to him, but after this I wanted to be done. I've never had a mom and I didn't want to do that to my baby. The bigger my stomach got, the more I just wanted to be a mommy. I didn't want my son to ever grow up and not know what it was like to have me in his life.

My ass was scared and not to go to war, but to be robbed of parenthood like my mama was. We had no idea what was in store for us and that had me thinking about my baby. That wasn't exactly what one should be thinking about when they are about to go into the unknown. I wanted to turn my car around, but we owed this to Glitch and Fat Back.

When this was done, I would allow my daddy to shoot me down. I know him like I know myself and there was no doubt in my mind that he would tell me I was out of the game. You could tell Capone wanted to say it now and they would work together to make it happen. What they didn't know was I would gladly give this shit up for my baby.

Besides, I was tired of having a power struggle with my daddy. This was what he wanted and he was back. My legacy wasn't going anywhere because I was my father's legacy. The Barnes would continue to run this city and I would get to be a mommy. If he ever needed me, I could easily go back and help him. Like an honorary boss.

Knowing it was time to get my mind on what was at hand, I turned on Chun Li by Nicki Minaj and blasted that shit until I was a block away from our destination. She wanted me to be the bad guy, well that's what the fuck I was about to be. Nobody fucked with my family and got away with that shit. It was time to end this. As long as Lisa wasn't sending us off, this shit was going to end today.

I know it was about to be a battle. Everyone wanted to be the person that actually took her out. Each of us had a valid reason of wanting to do it. Rebecca had a lot of enemies within us and all of us wanted a piece of her. Breezy was standing on behalf of Glitch, but out of all of us, I think Capone had the biggest pain in his heart. This was way more personal for him than the rest of us. She killed his fucking parents and then tried to take him out. Seeing him be the first out of the car, I knew he was ready. I think the only reason Vicious wasn't first was because of his foot. I bet he was cursing my ass out as we speak.

Getting out the car, everyone grabbed their weapons and walked inside. I was surprised that Capone let Shitz in on this, but he was here gun ready. I was even more surprised to find out this wasn't an ambush. I just knew that bitch Lisa was setting our ass up, but she actually delivered. You could hear moaning and there was no way someone was fucking if it was a sneak attack. Vicious started signaling and pointing to Capone. They rounded the corner first. When the rest of us came around, we were shocked.

"I always knew that you two were fucking. All these years I was like why Fernando taking orders from a bitch that use pump it up, but I couldn't say that because I thought you was my homie's mama. You freaky though. If I had known you like to eat ass, I would have let you get me together Ms. Parker." We laughed at Shitz, but that was a nasty sight to see. An old ass lady eating the ass of an old ass nigga. Then it hit me.

"Daddy, you said you fucked her. Did she eat your ass?" Everyone started laughing, but I was dead serious.

"Roulette, I will beat the hormones out of your ass. Don't play with me." Before we could finish our back and forth, Breezy had hit the bitch so hard she passed out. Not having a beef with Fernando, it wasn't personal with him. Raising my gun, I shot his ass in the head. Knowing I wouldn't get a chance to touch Rebecca, I sat down. I was tired as hell.

Watching them tie her up, I couldn't wait to see what they had planned for her. This bitch deserved everything and more. Vicious was practically drooling and I was about to ask did he want his ass ate, but I figured this wasn't the time. Capone had a different look in his eyes. I've never seen him like this before and it was turning me on. Putting rope around her face, he made her head tilt back and stay like that. Her legs were spread wide and I could have done without seeing her pussy all in my face, but it was interesting to see why they did it.

"I know how you are feeling, so this is how it will go. Breezy will start it off and do what she need to get her feelings out of the way, I'll go next, and then you can finish her off. Does that sound good?" My daddy made good decisions when it came to this.

"Sounds like a plan. Thank you." Capone looked grateful and I was glad my daddy did that for him. My ass would have just started doing what I wanted to. This why I knew it was better for him to lead. This was his life and he knew it better. Breezy took no time doing her part. Grabbing the drill my father had, she took it to the bitch's knees. The pain woke her ass up, but her head was tilted so she couldn't see what was going on.

My best friend had a dark side and I learned that on today. She drilled that bitch in every spot that Glitch could no longer use. Her hands were next, then she put it in the middle of her neck. If this hoe lived, she would sound like the bitch on them cigarette commercials. I used to smoke face ass. Knowing they didn't have that much time left, my daddy moved Breezy out of the way.

This shit was getting juicy and I almost wanted to join in. I didn't know they were going to go all dark and twisted. I've never killed like this and I would have loved to be a part of it. Vicious grabbed his knife and leaned down before her. I wish one of them cut her tongue out, because the screams were irritating the fuck out of me.

When he stuck that knife in her coochie, I almost felt bad for her ass. This nigga was in here making steaked catfish and I didn't know whether to throw up or be amazed. He was fucking the bitch with the knife. I'm sure it was tearing the flesh out that lil dry thang. She was barely hanging on and it was time to allow her to go see Jesus for herself. Capone grabbed a hammer and hit her across her neck.

He hit her so hard, I jumped. I had no idea what he was trying to do, but I would never want to die like that. Yeah, it was time for me to get out this life because these niggas were getting creative. It's like I needed to look away, but I couldn't. He continued to hit her until her head fell off her body. At that point, I could no longer hold in my vomit. I understood the hurt and the pain that he had in him, but I no longer wanted to piss him off anymore. This nigga was crazy.

"Yall got me fucked up if you think I'm not going to do shit. I want a piece of this hoe." Shit, pulled his dick out and started pissing on her before he shot her head. I didn't understand the point but he wanted to be included.

"Nigga I don't know how you piss with that lil ass dick. Stop shooting that lil shit and let's go. We didn't get to do shit either, but we ain't whipping out lil ass starter dicks. Let's go." Uncle E Way was going off and we all fell out. He was mad as hell Shitz pulled his lil ass dick out. It was time to go. We all could finally rest.

Chapter Twenty-Two

CAPONE

*E*ver since we killed Rebecca, I felt relief, but not closure. It's been three months, and it still felt like I was missing a piece to the puzzle. Something just wasn't sitting right with me and I hated it. I just couldn't figure out why she would want me dead. If she didn't like to do the foot work herself, who was she gone get to do it? Especially since she was about to try and take over the streets. I'm not cocky or anything, but I did my job well.

"Baby, we need to talk. Before we go out here with the family, I wanted to tell you first." Grabbing Shorty's hand, we sat down on the couch. Vicious' house was full because they were throwing her a baby shower. Breezy didn't want one because Glitch couldn't make it.

"What up Shorty?" The look on her face let me know it was serious.

"I know you and my father has been pushing for me to retire and I wanted to let you know that I am done. I'm going to turn everything over to my dad on today. I invited the crew and all and I'm just going to be a mommy. It means more to me than having shoot outs over simple shit. I want my child to get the life I had but with a mother. Even though I still chose the streets, my dad was in my life every step of the way. He didn't miss any important dates, or conversations. No matter what I went through, he was there. I want to be that for my son." She don't know how that made me feel.

That told me she had grown up. Nothing was more important than her family and I know in my heart she was the one. I wish I had parents to share this with, but all I had were them. It wasn't the same, but it was the hand I had been dealt. I was grateful to Vicious, but it was not the same. I never got to know my father and the woman I thought was my mother was responsible for both of my parents being dead. The only thing I was certain of was that I loved Shorty and my baby.

"Thank you. You don't know how much this means to me. It's not that she didn't think she could do both, but she chose us. She felt that we were more important and I would make sure she was straight for the rest of her life. I would die trying to give her the world behind the shit she just did.

"Yeah yeah yeah, I'm the shit I know. It feels weird without Breezy, but the show must go on. After we are done here, can you take me up there to see her. My damn ankles are swollen and my pussy is in pain. You haven't had sex with in days. Is it because I got baby pussy? You don't want me no more Cap?" I was lost on how the conversation switched to this. One minute we were happy and the next, she was yelling at me saying I didn't want her. Not knowing how to respond to her hormones, I sat there with my mouth open.

"Oh, now you ain't got shit to say? Close your fucking mouth before I put this big ass foot in your shit. Oh my God, it's my feet ain't it. You used to suck on my toes and I know you don't eat pork, but they just look like pork. That's all." Then the tears came. "I didn't mean to get pork rinds for toes. I'm sorry." I was about to grab her when her daddy walked in. He was looking pissed and I thought something had happened. As soon as we thought it was over, some more shit went down.

"If yall don't bring yall nasty asses out here and open these gifts. You know I don't like people at my house and they keep asking to tell stories from back in the day. Let's go."

"Okay, we're on the way now." Just like that, she stopped crying and walked out.

"What the fuck just happened?" Speaking out loud to myself, I walked out to join the rest of the party. I went from feeling happy to confused all in a few minutes. Everyone was having a good time and my Shorty was walking around looking good as fuck. You couldn't tell she was just inside having a break down. The smile on her face melted my heart and I wanted to always see her that way.

"Everyone I have an announcement to make. I am no longer returning to the game once my baby is born. Roulette will be no more, but don't worry. You will be in good hands. My daddy Vicious and my man Capone will be taking over for me. This is not tempo-rary and I will not change my mind. They got you and I want you to give them the same dedication you gave me." When everyone in the room started cheering on Vicious and me taking over, her face went from happy to sad.

"Fuck yall. You bitches been waiting to push me out? I'll make sure none of you get to work for them. What's the problem? Nobody wants to be seen or work with the big feet girl. I hate this entire house." She took off running and everyone gave me sympathetic looks. They knew how the hormonal shit works. They tried to tell me, but I didn't understand it would be this hard.

"Damn my nigga. Your shorty is ready to kill everyone out here. She ain't shit to play with. I'm surprised her crazy ass ain't take out your mama when she came in and tried to smother you with that pillow. As feisty as she is, I'm surprised she was able to hold off."

"That's not my mama and yea my Shorty crazy as hell. Quick question though. How you know my mother tried to smother me?" He looked confused and tried to figure out what the fuck I was saying. He wouldn't have to figure it out long though, I was going to tell him.

"What you mean? You told me."

"Naw, I told you she tried to kill me. I never told you how. So, is there something you want to tell me?"

"Bro, I don't think I like what you are implying. The fuck wrong with you?"

"Ain't shit wrong my nigga. I just want you to man up and tell me the truth. I already know you are flaw, what I want to know is what were you getting out of the deal. Ahhh, I see. She was giving you my seat." I couldn't stop laughing. Shitz wasn't smart enough to run an operation. She was going to make him her puppet and he didn't know. His ass wanted to be at the top so bad, he didn't even realize she played his ass.

"Cap, you my brother. I didn't know she was going to try and kill you. All she said was you were going to step down. That's it. You had Roulette and I thought you would be happy. Over the years, you have complained time and time again how you were tired of her and the life. I thought I was doing you a favor." Laughing, I pulled my gun. The yard got quiet and everyone was now staring at us.

"Nigga you think I give a fuck that you didn't know she was going to kill me. You're a snake and I don't do those. Now you can go work for her in hell bitch." Pulling the trigger, I shot him right between the eyes. Shorty walked out and screamed.

"Really. This what the fuck yall gone do at my baby shower. You could have at least told me you were killing our baby's God father. I know you're working against me. He probably liked my feet, so you killed him. Fuck you Capone." Everyone laughed, but this time she laughed with us. "I swear I hate this family."

"Aight, let's clean this shit up and continue on with the party. I ain't bring you niggas out here for nothing." Vicious started delegating and we listened. I could finally move on.

Chapter Twenty-Three

BREEZY

*T*hese have been the longest months of my life. Even though Glitch was happy about Rebecca being dead, he turned into a cold mean person. It's like I had my fiancé back, but he was not there. Most days he cursed me out and told me to just leave, but I would sit right there. No matter what the doctor's said, he wouldn't do the therapy and I was damn near over this shit.

I had no idea why I was going through so much pain, especially when we had the chance to be happy. He was choosing to be miserable and I didn't want to be on that ride. My ass cried damn near every night and his answer would be for me to get the fuck out. I didn't know how much more I could take and I had no one to talk to about this.

It's not that Roulette hadn't been here for me, I just didn't want her worrying about me. She was having an emotional pregnancy and I didn't want to worry her. This was my fight and I would just have to find a way to get through this on my own. Looking over at him, I attempted to have a good day with him. Glitch hadn't eaten and I wanted to feed him and talk to him about the baby. Grabbing a spoonful of his food, I put it to his mouth. Turning his face, he wouldn't take the food. The only thing he did was go off on my ass again.

"Get that nasty ass shit out of my face. Would you eat that shit or are you just trying to feed it to me because you think I deserve that shit?" The tears started to build up and I fought hard to keep them from falling.

"You don't have to talk to me like that, I'm just trying to help you. All I need you to do is try and we can move past this. Yelling is not going to make you better, I just want to help you get better."

"I DON'T NEED YOU TO HELP ME GET BETTER. The only reason you want me better is because you're embarrassed to be with someone like this. You don't have to be here and I'm telling you that I don't want you here."

"You know what, I don't have to take the shit that you are dishing out. I've tried my best to stay strong, but you are making this hard. I didn't give a fuck what happened to you, I just wanted to be with you. To have our family we fought for. If you don't want that, then fuck it. You win, I'm gone." Standing up, I attempted to storm out but a pain hit me out of nowhere. "Ahh fuck." Bending over, I couldn't stop the pain that was coming. It was unbearable. Screaming for help, the nurses came running in.

Glitch was screaming my name, but I couldn't answer him. All I could focus on was the nurse saying my baby was on the way. It wasn't time and my baby was making its way out. I know it was from the stress and me barely taking care of myself, but I had to make sure Glitch was okay. Mustering up enough strength to talk, I grabbed the nurse so she can hear me.

"Get my phone and call my best friend. I need her here please call her right now." Doing as I asked, I knew I would be okay. Roulette will be here and everything will go fine. There is no way God will allow me to lose two babies. This one had to make it. I felt bad because I didn't give her the nutrients that she needed. I was too involved in Glitch that I neglected my own personal needs.

The doctors rushed me off and I prayed that Roulette got here in time. I don't think I could make it through this without her. I don't know why God was hitting me with so much karma, but I was broken. I needed some good news to give me the push to go on. The tears fell as they prepped me and got me ready. I felt so alone and I wish I hadn't pushed my daddy away. If I hadn't did what I did to Glitch, he wouldn't have left the house. He would be in here with me if I hadn't pissed him off. All this was my fault. Now I was alone giving birth to my baby early.

"Bitch you better not push without me. You got me fucked up. I know yall I ain't think I was gone miss my God child being born. Come on bitch I need you to be strong and get the baby here." Smiling through my tears, I was happy as hell to hear her voice. Everything after that was a blur until the baby came. When I didn't hear crying, I broke down. I didn't want to live in a world with this much pain. I couldn't take anymore and I was done fighting.

Out of nowhere, I heard the cry and my heart felt so much relief. God loved me after all. He didn't leave me down here and abandon me. Thank you God. My baby is okay and fine. The joy that I felt in heart was unexplainable. The shit gave me new hope and I had something to keep fighting for. Whether Glitch wanted to be there or not, I had something to keep me going.

"Congrats mommy, your little girl is beautiful. Would you like to hold her?" Nodding my head yes, they brought her over to me. When I looked at Roulette, she was crying harder than me. It may have been the hormones, but either way, she was here sharing this moment with me. Grabbing my baby, I looked at her and she was a splitting image of Glitch. I wish he was here to see her it may have given him a reason to fight. Out of nowhere, we heard a commotion and I stopped to her what the hell was going on.

"I don't give a fuck what is going on. Let me in there to see my girl or I will blow this shit up. She needs me and I need to know that she is okay. GET ME IN THAT FUCKING ROOM." Me and Roulette laughed and it felt good to know that Glitch still cared.

"It's okay. He can come in and see her now. We're all done here." They wheeled him in and all I could do was smile. The look of worry on his face let me know that he was just talking shit.

Sighing a breath of relief, I started to get excited about my life. When they rolled him up to me, tears were in his eyes.

"Before you say anything, let me get this off my chest. The fact that you had to avenge me fucked me up. It bothered me that I couldn't be out there doing it myself. That shit hit my ego like a wave. Then you come back and you're trying to feed me and do everything for me, had me feeling like an invalid. You didn't even try to get me to work harder at getting better, you just did it as if you knew that was my life.

I didn't want you to help me. I wanted and needed you to push me. Then out of nowhere you started pushing me to hurry up and get better as if a life with me like that was unbearable. I understand that none of that is true because I know you. In my mind, at that time, that's what I thought. This shit fucked my head up, but I'm sorry that I took the shit out on you. I could have talked to you and I'm sorry."

"It's okay baby, I'm just glad you're here now. She looks just like you and this is the happiest day of my life. Thank you." He looked at me like it was more and I braced myself.

"Don't thank me yet. I was so mad at you, I wanted to punish you and... Well, I just want you to remember how happy you are now when I show you this." I had no idea what he was talking about, but my antennas were up like a mother fucker. When this lil irregular dick having ass nigga reached his hands up to grab the baby, I looked at him like he was crazy.

"You better be reaching for Jesus. You not about to drop my baby with those flimsy ass hands. You better not be telling me what I think you are." When he laughed and grabbed the baby out of my arms, a million emotions ran through me. Reaching my hand up, I slapped the smirk right off his face. He had me fucked up if he thought I wasn't about to get that lick off.

"You got that ma. What should we name her? I can't believe I have a daughter."

"I want to name her something simple and pretty. What about Alexia?"

"Shit is perfect."

"Aight, you bitches done got too mushy for me. I'm about to head out, I'll be back in a few. Don't kill each other before then." Roulette hugged us and went about her way. Even though I was mad at him from keeping this from me, I was happy. This was a perfect moment with a perfect baby and I wouldn't have it any other way. The storm was finally over.

Chapter Twenty-Four

VICIOUS

*W*ith all the shit that was going on, my ass felt like I had aged fifty fucking years. Kalina gave her crew over to me, but a nigga was tired. I know I couldn't give it up, but this shit we just went through was just too much. Especially finding out that Shitz was a snake. If we weren't at Kalina's baby shower, more would have been done to his ass.

That's the type of shit I don't like. You don't get to be in my crew and have a disloyal bone. That is the worst thing you could ever do to someone. I didn't give second chances, but I damn sure didn't play that flaw shit. On top of all the other shit we went through, Kalina was a handful. Kelly didn't go through emotions like this. All she did was crave crazy ass food. This was another level.

I didn't know what to say to her ass sometimes. The way she would cry will have your ass feeling like shit. Big ass dumb tears would be falling, then in a moment's notice, she would be laughing and asking for food. I didn't know whether I was coming or going with her sometimes, but I was enjoying most of it. There was no way I would have expected to be having a grandson this year and I couldn't wait until he came.

He was going to have what Kalina didn't. Two parents and a

grandfather. That was a blessing within itself. Just as I was smiling about my own grandbaby, the phone rang. Seeing it was my child, I prayed her ass wasn't having one of her meltdowns.

"What's up baby girl?" I could hear her crying and I took a deep breath. She was determined to wear my ass out.

"Breezy just went into labor early. I had to get some stuff, but I think you should come up. I know in this moment she is missing Fat Back and it would help to have you there." Not caring about anything else, I jumped up to head out of the door.

"Say less. I'm on the way." Running to the store, I grabbed a bunch of shit and headed up to the hospital. This is why I wanted her to have a baby shower with Kalina. Now her ass don't have shit and we had to hustle to make sure she was straight. Getting out of the car, I ran inside with all that I could carry and paid a nurse to get the rest. When I walked in the room, the family was there. I smiled because all of us had the same thought. Their room was packed with all kinds of shit.

"Hey, I hear I got a new baby girl. Let me see my bad ass baby. You know she gone be crazy just like her mama. Yes she is." Grabbing the baby, I couldn't stop myself from smiling. I had two grandbabies because I was standing in for Fat Back. There was no way I was letting her grow up without a grandparent.

"Alexia meet Paw Paw. Yup, that's your granddaddy. I know he is old, but that's all you got." Boo didn't know how good she made me feel when she said that. It's as if she read my mind and I was going to make her proud.

"Fuck you, I'm not old."

"He sure isn't. Hey you, do you have a moment." It was Melissa and I looked at Kalina to make sure she was good with it. Laughing, she shrugged her shoulders and I left out behind her. Pulling my hand, she dragged me all the way to the parking garage. I had no idea why we were down here, but I decided to go with the flow. Popping a lock on a truck, she climbed inside and I got in as well. When she started removing her scrubs, my dick bricked up instantly.

"Tell me what you did to that lady." I looked at her like she was crazy until she started playing in her pussy.

"First, we drilled holes in her legs and hands." The moans increased and I was turned on like a mother fucker.

"Fuck, do you hear how that pussy sounds. Keep talking."

"I fucked her with a knife cutting her shit up."

"Mmm like this." Sliding her finger in and out of her pussy, I would give anything to lick that shit off.

"Yeah, just like that. Then we hammered her head off her body." Her speed increased and I couldn't take it anymore. Snatching her up, I sat her on my lap. She was about to cum, but I wanted her to do that shit on my dick. I was tired of playing these games with her. Grabbing her around the waist, I slammed my dick inside of her. Within seconds, she was screaming and going crazy. That shit had me on edge, but I was Vicious. There was no way I was about to cum that fast. Not if I could help it. Wanting her to cum again, I kept talking.

"She was lucky, normally I would cut a nigga's tongue out, but it was nothing she could tell me. I wanted the bitch dead and we made her suffer bad. Blood was everywhere."

"Shit. I'm about to cum again." When her body started shaking, I knew I could finally release. Cumming inside of her, I grabbed her hand and sucked the juices off her finger."

"You keep acting like that, my ass gone be in love soon." Her shy demeanor came back and I didn't understand that shit. "Why are you so turned on by bad boys?" Getting dressed, she explained it to me the best she could.

"All my life, I did what my parents asked of me. I couldn't go to the hood. There was no time for parties. I had to be this image they had in their head of me. I followed the rules no matter what. I've always just wanted to do something wrong for once. I'm too scared to try anything on my own, so I always wanted to date someone that lacked fear. Who didn't care about being on the wrong side of the fence. I used to masturbate to what I thought a bad boy would do. Now that I have you, I can get the real thing and the shit just turns me on." I don't know why, but the shit was sexy as fuck and turned me on.

"Well, I got a lifetime of stories. Get over here and suck this dick while I tell you a few." Her mouth was so wet, I almost changed my mind. Fat Back called girls like her water babies. This water baby was about to get all this nut.

Once we were done, I headed upstairs and my ass had the limp. I don't know what this girl had pent up in her, but she was a beast. I've never had a girl fuck the shit out of me. My ass felt some kind of way and I'm glad we weren't lying down. I'm sure if we were in a bed, I would have tried to spoon and make breakfast in the morning.

My mind was fucked up and my dick was still hard. I had no idea how the fuck my dick was still hard, but it was. If my ego wasn't bruised, I would have fucked her again so I could try to win. This shit wasn't cool and we were gonna have to go another round when I left here tonight. When I got in the room, everyone was looking at me strange. Capone started laughing and I wanted to slap his ass out the window.

"I know that look. You got that she just fucked me into a coma walk going on. She just fucked you like you're the bitch and you liked it didn't you." I was about to laugh until reality hit me.

"Are you indirectly telling me about you and my daughter's sex life?" His laugh stopped immediately and we both were looking stupid.

"Well I'm not fucking your daughter and that is definitely the you got fucked look. Until you win, you are no longer in charge." Glitch was able to talk shit without feeling bad and I couldn't do shit but laugh.

"Fuck yall." Limping out the room, I went home to go to sleep.

Chapter Twenty-Five

BREEZY

I couldn't believe that the birth of my child brought my life back together. Everything was going perfectly and I had no idea how to handle it. I was scared to be happy because my happiness didn't last. Every time I thought I was on a good track, something would happen and I was back to where I started from.

Looking at Glitch doing his physical therapy had me smiling. He was determined to walk again so that he could be the best father he could be to our baby. That alone made me smile. This was all I wanted from the beginning and here he was walking on crutches trying to get back to a hundred percent. This was all I needed from him and I finally had it. My phone rung and I saw that it was Roulette.

"Hey bitch, Glitch ain't going nowhere and I need you to go look at this house with me. My daddy is great, but with this baby coming, me and Capone needed our own house. It's time to finally grow all the way up and I need my best friend to help me. Is that too much to ask for right now? I know that you're helping Glitch start back walking, but can you give me a few minutes?"

"Don't say it like he run me and shit. You can come get me and your niece. Just know that you are feeding me too. I'm not for your shit today. I have been eating nothing but fast food and I need a real meal. You got me?"

"You know I got your fat ass, but you gone have to try and get a lil cute. Your ass been looking a hot mess lately and I'm not going to a sit down restaurant with you looking like that. Now you have one hour to get your shit together."

"I hope you can't get your shoes on. Bye bitch." Hanging up, I jumped up and got ready the best I could. I was actually excited to get out of this place. It's been a long time since I went out and it felt good to finally get out of this place.

It didn't take me long to get ready, so I went back to Glitch to let him know me and the baby was leaving. The last thing I wanted was for him to think me and the baby was leaving him by his self. Even though I would never, his ass hasn't been here a day without me. Walking in the room, his ass was gone. Turning around, I stopped at the nurse's desk to find out where he was. After informing me that he was taking tests and it would be a few hours, I left to go make the run. By the time he got back, I should be done. When I got downstairs, Roulette was pulling up and that was perfect. When I got in the car, she had a weird look on her face.

"Come on bitch, why are you looking like that?"

"I'm waiting for the lady to text me back letting me know she was there. Calm down hoe, your ugly ass gone eat. I'm only taking you to Red Lobster, so you don't have to be in such a hurry."

"Next time you call and ask for my help, I'm not going to come. I don't have to take this shit from you. That's why my ankles went down and yours is still big as shit."

"Fuck you and you got throw up in your hair." While I tried to get the baby vomit out, she checked her phone and drove off. Usually, this bitch be driving like a bat out of hell in the Bugatti, but today she was barely moving. Something was off, but I had no idea what it was. When she was ready, she would tell me. It took us an hour to get to the house. If she was driving like she normally would, we would have gotten there in twenty five minutes. Getting out, I was jealous as hell of her. The house was beautiful and I knew that this was the one. I hadn't even seen the inside, but I knew that it had to be gorgeous. She walked me all over and I had tears in my eyes from the way that it looked.

It was the kind of house you wanted to settle down in. You would think she would get a mansion since that was what she was used to, but it was just a cozy beautiful Victorian Style house. Four bedrooms, two baths, and a gorgeous basement. Maybe I could get Glitch to find us one down the street.

"Last thing we need to see is the backyard. The baby would need a big yard." We headed out and it was so much space I started decorating it in my mind. Turning around to head back in, Glitch was kneeling with the help of a nurse.

"When you tied me up and beat me like I was a field nigga, I was leaving out every day to build you this house. Well I didn't build it, but I made sure they did the shit right. I would never cheat on you and I couldn't believe you thought it was another woman.

When I left out, I wasn't mad at you, but I wanted to hurry up and finish this shit so you could shut the fuck up. I was taken and you never got to know my plans. I asked you to marry me already, but after everything that has happened, I need to know you still want to. Would you still be my wife and share this house with me?" Running over to him, I jumped in his arms causing him to fall. He screamed out in pain and I felt like shit.

"I'm sorry baby and yes. Yes, I will marry you."

"If you keep this shit up, I won't be able to walk down the fucking aisle. Damn. You have to chill out baby. I'm healing and you trying to fuck up my progress."

"Yeah bitch. Do you know how hard it was to convince them to let his ass out? Be careful before your ass be a bitch pushing her nigga in a wheel chair. You know how hard it is to have a baby and a grown ass nigga in a stroller?" I was so happy, all I could do was laugh. With tears in my eyes, I helped him up and kissed him.

"Baby, I don't care if I have to push you down the aisle. All I want is you and I don't care about anything else. Me and my baby will love you no matter what. You are my everything and I am so sorry that you are going through this because of me. I never apologized, but it's my fault. If I hadn't did that to you that day, you wouldn't have left and you would have paid attention. Thank you for loving me enough to come back."

"Yeah, it is your fault. I didn't want to say shit, but now that you brought it up I'm just saying." I couldn't believe he agreed with me even though I knew he was joking. It was some seriousness in his tone and I knew I had fucked up. We were getting past it and that's all that matters.

"Okay, I know you all are having a beautiful moment, but we have to go. I promised them that I would have you back and I don't want to piss them off. They have been real lenient with us and all the visitors. I don't want to mess that up. Now bring your crippled, flappy dick ass on. You too with your funky ass. I told you to get pretty and you throw clothes on over the funk. Bring yall fucked up asses on."

"Fuck you." Me and Glitch said it at the same time. It felt good that the crew was all back together. Different, but together nonetheless. This was the best day of my life and I couldn't wait to marry my man.

Chapter Twenty-Six

ROULETTE

*I*t felt good to see everyone getting their happy ending. I had the perfect man, with the perfect baby on the way. Breezy had the perfect family and moving into her dream house. I don't know why they would want to give up the mansion, but I guess. Thinking it over, I guess it was time for me and Capone to do the same. There was no way all of us was going to work out living together.

I hadn't even thought about it before now and I needed to talk to Capone about this. Him and my daddy was getting very close, and although that was nice, he needed to know that we still were getting the fuck out of here. I found him in the kitchen in deep thought. Walking up to him, I hugged him. It felt good to hold him.

"Baby, I know you like it here, but we have to go when the baby is born. This shit is not going to work out. I know this is sudden and you don't have to build me a house like Glitch did for Breezy, but we need to get the fuck up out of here. Are you okay with that?"

"I don't think your father will be ready for that. Let's just have this baby first and see how it goes. It's been perfect for now and all he talks about is his grandson. I don't want to take that from him. You can't be that fucked up to do him like that." Pissed that he would say it like I was selfish, I allowed my emotions to get the best of me and I slapped him. He moved quick enough so that it wasn't hard, but I could see in his eyes he was pissed off.

"I see your ass just ain't gone learn. I'm tired of trying to tell you this shit and you're going to lose me. In the meantime, I'm about to make you feel some serious pain since your ass determined to keep putting your hands on me. Bend over."

"Okay, I'm sorry. I promise I didn't mean it. I won't do it again okay. Just wait a minute." He pushed my ass on the counter like I wasn't saying shit. Snatching my pants down, I prayed he didn't go in my ass. I heard something move around and then he flicked his lighter. I had no idea what was going on, but I was scared out of my mind. When I felt this heat hit my ass, I damn near jumped over the counter. Holding me down, he continued to pour. Tears in my eyes had me ready to fight him like he's never felt until I felt his dick go inside of me.

It was a painful pleasure that had me going crazy. The shit hurt like hell, but I wanted more. I needed more. It's like he knew I was liking it because he started slamming harder inside of me. It's like he wanted it to be painful for me and my freaky ass was ready to throw it back. Trying my best, he took control and continued to beat my shit up.

"That's right nigga punish this pussy. This cat needs a spanking. Wrarrr daddy fuck this cat up." My ass started going crazy and I needed to nut. My shit started building up and I came like I never have before. Even when I was done, his ass kept right on pounding. My insides started shifting and I could no longer keep up. He came long and hard and I was ready to go lay my ass down to sleep.

"What yall doing woke? Oh hell naw, you have got to be kidding me. Yall gotta get the fuck out of my house. The only nigga that can fuck in my kitchen is me. When yall moving? I need yall to start looking and get the fuck up out of here nasty ass bitches." Laughing, I knew I didn't have to worry about convincing Capone to move now. Out of nowhere, a bunch of water came out of me. They were talking shit back and forth ignoring me calling them.

"If you two don't shut the fuck up and take me to the hospital.

I'm in labor dumb asses." They both started panicking grabbing dumb shit and I stood there speechless. "Why the fuck would I need a food bag. WHY ARE YOU PACKING ME SNACKS? If you don't grab me and take me to the car, I will kick both of yall ass."

"Okay, let's go. Shit, you act like we know what the fuck we are doing. I was watching a movie and the guy packed snacks. I guess her big ass was hungry." The look I gave my father could have killed roaches. He had me fucked up.

"Did you just call me fat? I know the fuck you didn't just call me fat." Capone knew that my daddy fucked up and give him the come on before we die look. We headed out the door to go have a baby.

My father got us there in no time and I'm glad that he did. It felt like the baby was about to fall out of my ass and I needed it out of me now. That was all I wanted was for this baby to get out of me. They were talking and taking their time and I was about to die. Please God, I'm sorry for everything I have ever done. Please don't take it out on my coochie.

"Capone tell them to get the baby out of me right now. I need the baby out of me. Please. It hurt so bad, don't let them do this to me."

"Hurry up and help my Shorty before we have a problem. I don't want her to feel an ounce of pain and you need to fix it right now." They all started to move faster and I was grateful for him. We rushed in the room and thankfully it all went fast from there. They had me on the table prompting me to push, and I froze. That's how my mother died and it just hit me. What if the same thing happened to me while I was on the table pushing? My dad and Capone was looking at me like I was crazy, but I couldn't do this.

"Stop. I'm not pushing. Mom died like this and I can't do it daddy. Please don't make me do it. Oh God, I'm not ready to die and I can't push." I started crying and the panic set in. I couldn't breathe and nothing they did would calm me. It felt like I was dying from suffocation and my ass couldn't breathe.

"We are going to have to perform an emergency C Section. Call downstairs for an OR." When they said that, my head popped up and I calmed down right quick.

"I'm fine, I'll push."

"You so damn extra." My daddy was laughing, Capone was trying to see if I'm okay. Seeing me breathing right and pushing before they told me to, let him know I was good. Before I knew it, my baby boy was in my arms looking just like me. I'm glad that he took after me because Breezy baby didn't look like him at all. This little boy was all me and I was loving it. My daddy cried harder than I did and Capone was in shock. This was a happy moment and I couldn't wait to get him home. My son. This was my son.

"Just so you know, he is not taking your name. I want him to be his own person. His name is going to be Christian."

"I like that. How did you come up with that?" Capone thought it had some profound meaning.

"Off the soap opera One Life To Live."

"Something is seriously wrong with you."

"I love you both with all of my heart. Don't you ever forget it."

"I love you too baby girl."

"You know I love that fat ass umm. My bad. I love you too Shorty." Closing my eyes, this was the best feeling in the world.

Epilogue

$\mathcal{E}$verything had been going perfect in all of our lives. Nothing could take us off the high we had been on. My father was happy and in a relationship with Melissa, for some reason she got him. That girl loved him, dark side and all. Everything about him, she accepted and he needed that. Not someone trying to change who he was.

He was now running the crew with Capone as his connect and they worked perfectly together. They made sure that they made it home every day. If something came up, one would come home while the other figure out the problem. I was never left alone. This is how my daddy wanted it and he refused to take no for an answer.

Breezy and Glitch were the happiest couple I ever seen. They moved into their new house and my niece was getting big. They had gotten married and of course I was the Maid of Honor. It was the prettiest wedding I had ever seen. I cried the entire time and I can say it was from pure happiness. Glitch was back to normal and that was the biggest blessing of it all.

Me and Capone was in love, but I didn't want to jump into marriage. My father was pissed about it, but it wasn't his decision to make. I needed to know for sure without a doubt that we would never leave each other, no matter what. Even though I love him with all of my heart, I had to be sure. He was my everything, but if he tried to walk away, his ass was dead. Everything was perfect except for one final step.

Even though everyone thing had settled down and I stepped away from the life, it was one last thing I had to handle. No one knew I was here because they would have tried to stop me. My daddy would have panicked thinking I was back in the game and that was not the case.

I had to go to an outside source in order to get the information and now I was sitting outside the house. This was what I needed to make sure all of our skeletons were out of the closet. This was the only way I knew how to do that. Reaching in my glove box, I grabbed my special gun and got out. Pulling my hood down low, I walked to the house and picked the lock. Heading inside, I went to the bedroom. It was late as hell and I assumed they would be sleep.

Cutting on the light, I waited for them to adjust their eyes. Staring at me with fear all over face was Lisa. The bitch thought she could walk away from this, but that wasn't the case. I never forgot that it was her that told that bitch where we stayed and had Rebecca shooting at my daddy. She was the real reason Fat Back was gone. Her ass didn't get to walk away from this.

"Kalina, what are you doing here?"

"I was just wondering, are you feeling lucky?"

THE END...

KEEP UP WITH LATOYA NICOLE

Like my author page on fb @misslatoyanicole
My fb page Latoya Nicole Williams
IG Latoyanicole35
Twitter Latoyanicole35
Snap Chat iamTOYS
Reading group: Toy's House of Books
Email latoyanicole@yahoo.com

Other Books By Latoya Nicole

NO WAY OUT: MEMOIRS OF A HUSTLA'S GIRL

NO WAY OUT 2: RETURN OF A SAVAGE

GANGSTA'S PARADISE

GANGSTA'S PARADISE 2: HOW DEEP IS YOUR LOVE

ADDICTED TO HIS PAIN (STANDALONE)

LOVE AND WAR: A HOOVER GANG AFFAIR

LOVE AND WAR 2: A HOOVER GANG AFFAIR

LOVE AND WAR 3: A HOOVER GANG AFFAIR

LOVE AND WAR 4: A GANGSTA'S LAST RIDE

CREEPING WITH THE ENEMY: A SAVAGE STOLE MY HEART 1-2

I GOTTA BE THE ONE YOU LOVE (STANDALONE)

THE RISE AND FALL OF A CRIME GOD: PHANTOM AND ZARIA'S STORY

THE RISE AND FALL OF A CRIME GOD 2: PHANTOM AND ZARIA'S STORY

ON THE 12TH DAY OF CHRISTMAS MY SAVAGE GAVE TO ME

A CRAZY KIND OF LOVE: PHANTOM AND ZARIA

14 REASONS TO LOVE YOU: A LATOYA NICOLE ANTHOLOGY

SHADOW OF A GANGSTA

THAT GUTTA LOVE 1-2

LOCKED DOWN BY HOOD LOVE 1

LOCKED DOWN BY HOOD LOVE 2

THE BEARD GANG CHRONICLES 2 (THE TEASE)

THROUGH THE FIRE: A STANDALONE NOVEL

DAUGHTER OF A HOOD LEGEND

Book 26!!!!!!

BOOK 26, AND I CAN'T BELIEVE IT. NINE NUMBER ONES, I'M STILL IN DISBELIEF. YOU GUYS ARE AWESOME, AND I LOVE YOU. THANK YOU FOR CONTINOUSLY MAKING MY BOOKS A SUCCESS. WITHOUT YOU THERE IS NO ME. MAKE SURE YOU DOWNLOAD, SHARE, READ AND REVIEW. MORE BOOKS WILL BE COMING FROM ME. BE ON THE LOOK OUT. NO MATTER WHAT HAPPENS, I HOPE YOU ALL WILL CONTINUE TO SUPPORT ME THE SAME. NO MATTER WHAT, I'M STILL LATOYA NICOLE. IT CAN ONLY GET BETTER.

CPSIA information can be obtained
at www.ICGtesting.com
Printed in the USA
LVHW011807271018
595053LV00023B/305/P